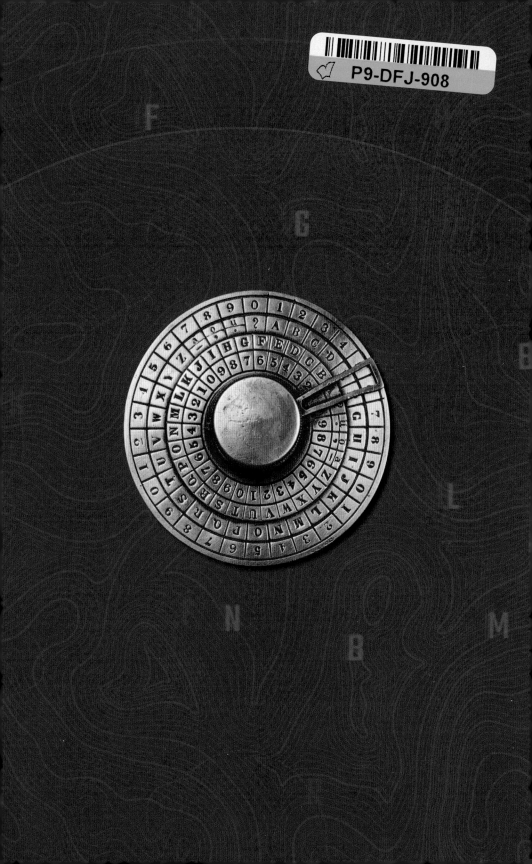

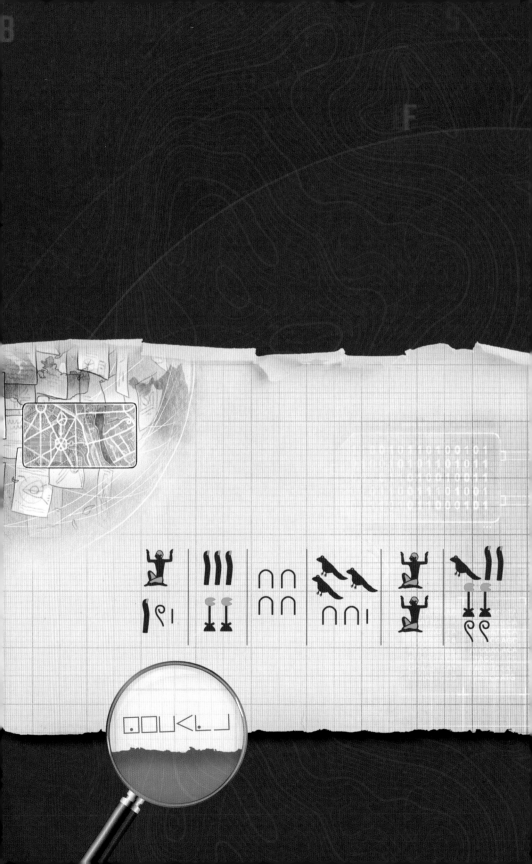

NATIONAL
GEOGRAPHIC

EXPL⬥RER
ACADEMY

CODE-
BREAKING
ACTIVITY ADVENTURE

DR. GARETH MOORE

NATIONAL GEOGRAPHIC

WASHINGTON, D.C.

CONTENTS

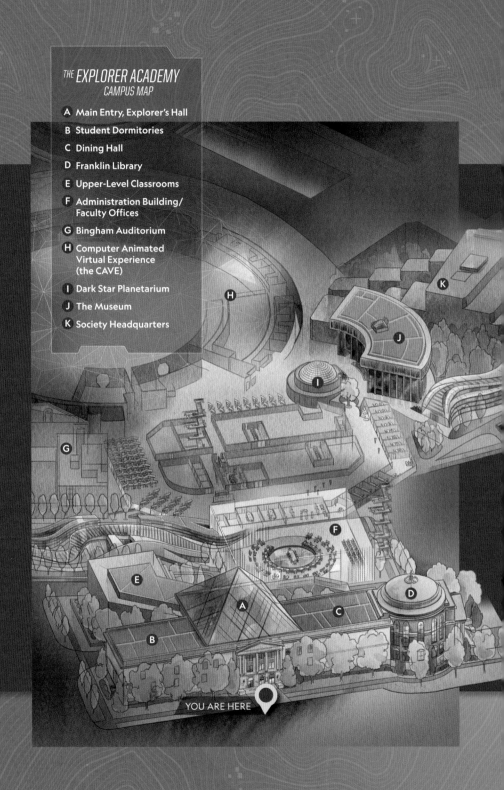

THE EXPLORER ACADEMY
CAMPUS MAP

A Main Entry, Explorer's Hall

B Student Dormitories

C Dining Hall

D Franklin Library

E Upper-Level Classrooms

F Administration Building/
Faculty Offices

G Bingham Auditorium

H Computer Animated
Virtual Experience
(the CAVE)

I Dark Star Planetarium

J The Museum

K Society Headquarters

YOU ARE HERE

EXPLORER ACADEMY

Greetings, new recruit! Congratulations on your recent acceptance to our elite Explorer Academy!

Welcome to headquarters. Inside these hallowed halls, you will follow in the footsteps of great explorers of the past, as you are one of the great innovators of the future. We select prospective candidates of only the highest merit to receive this opportunity, so we are confident that you are up to the great challenges that lie ahead. Your training begins ... now!

Your first challenge will be the annual explorer scavenger hunt. This unique series of missions will test your codebreaking skills as you work your way through head-scratching puzzles designed to outwit even the most clever of cryptographers. But if you successfully navigate the challenges, you will get a first-class tour of the society—and maybe even uncover some areas not generally available to students. (However, for your own protection, I must caution you to stay away from anywhere labeled "off-limits.")

Everything you need to know can be found in the enclosed book. Turn the page when you are ready to begin. And remember, this is just the beginning of your adventure. As a student at the Academy, you will enjoy the rare privilege of learning firsthand from a faculty of the world's most renowned scientists, explorers, conservationists, photographers, and journalists as you travel to historic and majestic locations around the globe.

Above all—have fun!

Cordially,

Regina M. Hightower, Ph.D.
Explorer Academy President

// MESSAGE FROM TARYN //

Dear Explorer,

Welcome to D.C.! I hope you had a pleasant journey. Allow me to introduce myself. My name is Taryn, and I'm your dorm adviser. You can usually find me and Hubbard, my terrier, either at the Academy's front desk or in my room on the fifth floor—the Sahara room.

You are now ready for <u>your</u> first challenge.

This scavenger hunt will take you on a <u>journey</u> through a world of ciphers (secret codes), where we <u>will</u> reveal hidden messages and secret symbols. You will <u>start</u> to understand the mysteries hidden within the ordinary everyday text found <u>in</u> all kinds of books and other writings.

<u>The</u> most important lesson you will learn is to pay attention to anything out of the ordinary—and be sure to use the <u>library</u> for assistance, if needed. (You may also consult the solutions at the back of this handbook if you get really stuck.)

So, where do you start? You were chosen for the Academy because you stand out from the crowd; are there any words in this letter that also stand out from the rest? The answer to this question will tell you where to begin.

Good luck!
Taryn Secliff
Dorm Adviser

/ CODE 1.1 /

 This letter is telling you where to go to begin your scavenger hunt. Read the words that "stand out," in the order that they appear. What do they say?

< / WRITE YOUR DESTINATION BELOW / >

WHAT IS CODEBREAKING?

People have been sending secret messages for thousands of years. Whether to outsmart an enemy or to communicate private data or just to swap for-your-eyes-only notes with their pals, clever code-makers have created lots of different types of cipher—ways of transforming information to hide its true meaning. Coded letters, numbers, and symbols often look familiar, but their precise arrangement is used to conceal a hidden message.

As you journey through the Academy, you'll become familiar with all kinds of ciphers—from the ancient Greek Polybius square to the cool clicks of Morse code. Some ciphers can be cracked with only a little bit of effort and some creative thinking. Others, however, need special knowledge of the steps taken to create them. No matter the challenge, instructions and helpful hints will point you in the right direction along the way.

NEED A HINT?

Don't worry—Hubbard's here to help! Look for his furry face or paw print along your journey if you need an extra clue. For example, stumped on Taryn's message? Here's your clue:
{ HUBBARD'S HINT } READ ONLY THE UNDERLINED WORDS.

<THE LIBRARY>

Welcome to your first mission.

Congratulations on cracking your first code! You've successfully revealed the first hidden message by reading only the underlined words.

Now that you have proven your ability, your scavenger hunt will really begin! Sitting ***on*** a desk before you is your first test: a thick book, packed full of codes! Only by ***cracking*** each code will you reveal a new hint to continue ***your*** challenge.

Don't be confused if at ***first*** the solution to each challenge seems to make little sense. All will become clear at the end of the book, where each of your ***code*** solutions will be assembled together to reveal an overall hidden message. The answers that you have gathered will then tell you where to head next.

Now read each page carefully for instructions on how to solve ***the next*** code on that particular ***page***—or if you are feeling really brave, you could have a go at cracking the code without reading the instructions!

MISSION=1

Franklin Library

/ CODE 1.2 /

Some of the words in this coded message are *italicized*. Can you figure out what they're trying to tell you?

< / WRITE THE HIDDEN MESSAGE HERE / >

{ IMPORTANT TIP } Did you notice that there was no punctuation in the hidden sentence on the previous page? This will be a common feature of the codes you will be cracking, so you'll need to keep this in mind as you make your way through the challenges that lie ahead!

TIME TO GET STARTED! Words don't need to be visually highlighted to form a secret code. They could just be in the same position within a sentence. For example, is the passage below just about sports, or is there more to it?

CODE 1.3

Pay special attention to the last word of each sentence. Read together, in order, they will spell out part of a question that you will use for the final challenge in this chapter.

Sports and games tournaments have been popular throughout history, but the most exciting part of any tournament is often its final. This is where the eventual winner is decided, whether it is for a football tournament championship, an athletic event, or a spelling bee that comes down to its last letter.

The reason to participate in any of these events is usually, of course, mainly about having fun and joining in. Winning is not always an end in itself, but simply a fun goal to have while learning to throw the ball well, to run efficiently, or to learn all the ins and outs of the alphabet.

< / WRITE THE SECRET MESSAGE HERE / >

GREAT, ON TO THE NEXT CODE! Sentences can group words together in meaningful ways. These help us understand what has been written much more easily than if the words just flowed together without any breaks. Sentences also often take up multiple lines, simply because we run out of room to write all the words on a single line. The place where the sentence stops and moves down to the next line—called a line break—is usually random and not important.

However, line breaks do have a special meaning when they appear in poetry—have you ever read a haiku?—and they can have a special meaning in a coded message, too.

CODE 1.4

At first, this page just seems to contain jokes and puns. Wait a second—check out the first word of each line. Read together, in order, they reveal a hidden question you'll need to answer later.

What do you call a one-eyed dinosaur?

Is an alligator in a vest an investigator?

The sleeping bull was a bulldozer.

Fifth place was V good to the Romans.

Vowel, towel, foul, and trowel all contain two vowels.

< / WRITE THE HIDDEN QUESTION HERE / >

ANSWER: A ONE-EYED DINOSAUR IS A "DO-YOU-THINK-HE-SAURUS," AND FIFTH PLACE WAS "V," GOOD TO THE ROMANS BECAUSE "V," IS THE ROMAN NUMERAL FOR 5!

SOMETIMES, THE SECRET WORDS OR LETTERS IN A CODE ARE HIDDEN and will not be directly highlighted. This can make them trickier to spot.

CODE 1.5

Below is a photocopy from a popular book in the Academy library. Some sections of the text have been highlighted to make it look as if someone has read it and then taken notes. Instead of paying attention to the highlighted sections themselves, however, read the first word after each highlighted section to reveal a secret question you'll need to answer later.

The first human to travel into outer space was the Russian cosmonaut Yuri Gagarin. His spacecraft completed an orbit of the Earth in April 1961, which made him an international celebrity.

Despite his amazing feat, he carried on his work as a test pilot, which ultimately led to his death in 1968, when his aircraft crashed. A letter he wrote just two days before his famous 1961 flight was then given to his widow, in which he wrote about what should happen if he were to crash. It sounds like it was written because he thought that his original spaceflight might not be successful, but in a carefully coded way—most likely because he did not want the government of the day to censor it.

Gagarin was originally chosen for his space mission as the candidate his colleagues would most like to see go into space, perhaps because of his famous smile. Crowds would come to see him wherever he traveled.

< / WRITE THE SECRET QUESTION HERE / >

TO REVEAL THE HIDDEN MESSAGE ON THIS PAGE
you'll need more than just words—you'll also need a picture!

CODE 1.6

Take a look at this drawing of the center of the constellation Ursa Major. Seven of its stars make up the famous Big Dipper. See how they can be connected to reveal a shape?

The picture below has the same stars, but this time there are words instead of the lines that made up the constellation. This second picture conceals a secret message. Can you figure out how to use the star chart to reveal that message?

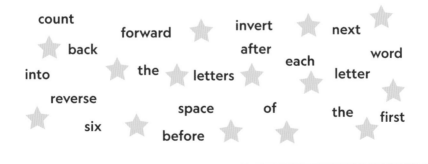

< / WRITE THE SECRET MESSAGE HERE / >

{ HUBBARD'S HINT } IF YOU COPY THE LINES FROM THE STAR CHART, THE LINES THAT MAKE UP THE BIG DIPPER WILL CROSS THROUGH SIX WORDS. READ THESE SIX WORDS IN ORDER, FROM THE LEFT TO THE RIGHT OF THE CONSTELLATION, TO REVEAL A HIDDEN MESSAGE YOU WILL NEED LATER.

IN CODES CALLED ACROSTICS, only certain letters in each line are meant to be read. These individual letters are then combined to form a word or words. The simplest type of acrostic is formed by taking the first letter of each line and then reading these together. For example, an acrostic reading of this paragraph would be IMTTWHS. In this case, the result is nonsense because there is no hidden acrostic in it. But if you try the same technique with the text below, you should find a different result!

CODE 1.7

You turn the page to find an oddly typed paragraph. Can you read the acrostic message? It is a question with five separate words.

Whenever you need
Help or some kind of
Assistance with a puzzle,
Turn to your friendly,
Inspirational librarian for
Some clever help and
Thoughtful ideas. It's a
Huge relief to know that
Every time you enter
This room you are back
Home with so many
Internationally famous and
Renowned books, including

Those that might then
Even help you answer the
Enigmas, the conundrums, the
Nagging questions, and
The other problems you
Have been recently
Looking at trying to
Eventually solve, so
That at the end of
The day you can go home
Early with your work all
Reliably completed.

< / WRITE THE HIDDEN MESSAGE HERE / >

READY FOR BIGGER CHALLENGES? All the codes you've cracked so far have involved reading words or letters directly from a message. Most real-world codes are trickier than this, however, and involve changing the message first. This might involve rearranging letters or words in some way. There are lots of different ways of doing this, and you'll learn about some of these over the next few pages.

CODE 1.8

The sentence below might look like nonsense, but in fact only some simple changes have been made to it. Can you figure out what has happened? Think about swapping letters around; you won't have to move any individual letter very far.

ESRCTE OCEDS AHEV FOETN
EBNE SUDE OT ESDN MIOPTRNAT
EMSSGASE UDIRGN ITEMS FO AWR.

< / WRITE THE DECODED MESSAGE HERE / >

{ HUBBARD'S HINT } THE SECRET HERE IS TO CONSIDER *PAIRS* OF LETTERS WITHIN EACH WORD—WHETHER, SAY, THE FIRST AND SECOND LETTER IN EACH WORD HAVE BEEN SWAPPED, AND THEN THE THIRD AND FOURTH LETTERS (IF THERE ARE FOUR OR MORE LETTERS) HAVE BEEN SWAPPED, AND SO ON. IF YOU DIDN'T CRACK THE CODE ALREADY, USE THIS INFORMATION TO FIGURE OUT WHAT IT SAYS: THE FIRST WORD DECODES TO "SECRET."

LETTERS CAN BE REARRANGED in many different ways in a code, some of which are more complex than others.

In the code on this page, the letters in each word are written in a different order than normal, but the order is a fairly easy one to guess.

CODE 1.9

There is just one sentence here. Can you figure out what it says? If you get stuck, try looking at each word from a different angle.

NAC UOY LLET EM TAHW EHT ELDDIM RETTEL FO EHT DROW "TRA" SI?

< / WRITE THE DECODED QUESTION HERE / >

{ HUBBARD'S HINT } STILL FEELING BACKWARD? TRY COPYING OUT EACH WORD BUT WITH ITS LETTERS REVERSED. DID THAT TURN IT AROUND FOR YOU?

WORDS CAN ALSO BE REARRANGED to make a hidden message!
    If you were able to decipher the code on the previous page, you are ready to tackle the one here, too. It works in a very similar way, but it's now words instead of letters that have been rearranged.

CODE 1.10

What does this message say?

CODEBREAKER MASTER A BECOMING ARE YOU! CRYPTOGRAPHER A CALLED IS CODES ON EXPERT AN.

< / WRITE THE DECODED MESSAGE HERE / >

 { HUBBARD'S HINT } HAVE YOU TRIED
READING EACH SENTENCE BACKWARD?

IN THE CODES YOU'VE CRACKED SO FAR, you've been able to read the answer directly from the text by using the appropriate decoding steps. In some codes, however, you also need to apply some detective work to extract the original, hidden message. Are you up for it, explorer?

CODE 1.11 /

The message below has had all of its spaces deleted. Not so complicated, right? But to make things more challenging, they've been added back in at random! This means that most or all of them are now in the wrong place, and there may be the wrong number of spaces, too.

Can you rearrange the spaces to figure out what it originally said?

WHI CHLE TTE ROFT HEAL PHAB ETLO OKSMOSTLI KEAP ERF ECTCI RCLE?

< / WRITE YOUR DECODED QUESTION HERE / >

CERTAIN LETTERS OR WORDS IN A SECRET MESSAGE

may sometimes be missing completely. This makes the message much more secret, but it also means that you will need to figure them out for yourself. This might sometimes involve some guessing, but if you use your superior skill and judgment, explorer, you should be able to restore enough of the missing words or letters to make sense of the original message.

The best way to tackle this type of hidden message is to work your way through the entire code, without stopping for too long on any parts you can't yet crack. Sometimes the bits you do figure out will then afterward help you make sense of the parts you were stuck on. In other words, if you are stuck at the start of a sentence then try the middle and end instead; cracking a later part might help you with an earlier bit.

CODE 1.12

Can you figure out what is written below? Every vowel has been replaced with a # symbol.

WH#T #S TH# N#N#T##NTH L#TT#R #F TH# #LPH#B#T?

< / WRITE YOUR DECODED QUESTION HERE / >

{ HUBBARD'S HINT } THE FIRST WORD IS "WHAT." IF YOU NEED ANOTHER HINT, THE MISSING VOWELS ARE AIEIEEEEEOEAAE.

WHEN YOU HAVE A CODE THAT REQUIRES SOME GUESSWORK, it becomes much harder to crack. Someone trying to figure out your code could easily be stuck if they don't have the same knowledge that you do.

One way to conceal words is just to scramble the letters. Too easy? Well, if you want to do this *and* disguise that you've done so, you could try scrambling them up to make new words.

In the coded text below, all the words or phrases are scrambles of animal names. Ignore any spaces, so for example, "Horn or ices" would be a way of hiding "rhinoceros." The coded and decoded text use the same set of letters, just in a different order.

CODE 1.13

First, unscramble the following animals, writing your answers on the blank lines:

1. PET ALONE _____
2. RAPTOR _____
3. IS TORCH _____
4. EPHES _____
5. RE TIG _____

6. NEER RIDE _____
7. COP OUTS _____
8. PINE GUN _____
9. SHORE _____
10. NEAT HELP _____

Then, once you have discovered each of the hidden animals, read down the first letter of each animal, as in an acrostic code, to reveal a 10-letter word.

< / WRITE THE SOLUTION HERE / >

{ HUBBARD'S HINT } THE ANIMALS INCLUDE SHEEP, HORSE, PARROT, TIGER, PENGUIN, OSTRICH, ANTELOPE, ELEPHANT, OCTOPUS, AND REINDEER.

LETTER REARRANGEMENT CODES DON'T NEED TO BE AS COMPLEX as a complete scramble of all of the letters. They could, for example, simply involve swapping a single pair of letters in each word.

CODE 1.14

Can you figure out what the following fact says?

TI SAW EHT GODEBREAKINC SKILLS FO POT SRYPTOGRAPHERC THAT DELPEH EHT SLLIEA OT NIW EHT DECONS DORLW RAW.

< / WRITE THE DECODED FACT HERE / >

{ HUBBARD'S HINT } THE SECOND WORD IS NOT "SAW." IT DECODES TO READ "WAS."

YOU'RE ALMOST AT THE END

of the book of codes and the first leg of your code-cracking journey, explorer! You vaguely notice Cruz's honeybee drone, Mell, buzzing nearby, but you have to stay focused.

In the code on the previous page, the first and last letters of each word were swapped. A similar code can be created that works in the opposite way, where the first and last letters remain unchanged but all of the other letters are swapped around. All the words have been changed in exactly the same way.

CODE 1.15

Can you make sense of this coded message?

WAHT IS THE TRIHD CNANOSNOT IN THE ESILGNH AEBAHPLT?

< / WRITE THE DECODED QUESTION HERE / >

{ HUBBARD'S HINT } REMEMBERING THAT THE FIRST AND LAST LETTERS REMAIN UNCHANGED, TRY REVERSING THE ORDER OF ALL THE OTHER LETTERS IN EACH WORD. THIS MEANS, FOR EXAMPLE, THAT THE FIFTH WORD WILL NOW BE "CONSONANT."

WORDS WITH MISSING VOWELS are often still possible to read. For example, "hppy" can be read as "happy" (or "hoppy," or even "hippy") easily enough—which of the three options it is should usually be clear from the words surrounding it.

But what if a coded message had been created by swapping the vowels around, so that A had become E, E had become I, I had become O, O had become U, and U had become A?

Surprisingly, this makes it harder to guess what the original word should be, because it stops your brain from automatically supplying a likely vowel—at least until you stop and carefully figure it out.

CODE 1.16

Using this vowel-swapping code, try decoding the following message. Remember that to decode the message you will need to *undo* the vowel swapping that has already taken place.

WHET LITTIR EPPIERS THORD MUST FRIQAINTLY ON THOS PHRESI?

< / WRITE THE DECODED QUESTION HERE / >

As you finish the book's last page, Mell drops a piece of paper in front of you. It's your final code!

{ HUBBARD'S HINT } TO REVEAL THE ORIGINAL TEXT, YOU'LL NEED TO CHANGE EACH A TO U, EACH E TO A AND SO ON.

CONGRATULATIONS, EXPLORER–

YOU HAVE COMPLETED THE FIRST SET OF CODEBREAKING MISSIONS. Now it's time to check your code-cracking abilities and put your skills to the test by combining the answers from your previous codes. Doing so will reveal the next location at which you can continue your scavenger hunt. Even master codebreakers can't crack every code, however. So if you don't have all the answers you need, you can always check the solutions at the back of the book.

CODE 1.17

Some of the answers to the previous puzzles have described things, so you should write in the boxes below whatever it is that they describe. For example, if your answer read "first letter in alphabet," then write an *A* in the box.

The next location is described by a three-word phrase:

WORD 1

☐ = letter that answers the secret question in code 1.5

☐ = letter that answers the decoded question in code 1.9

☐ = letter that answers the hidden question in code 1.4

☐ = letter described by the secret message in code 1.3

☐ = punctuation symbol representing the solution in code 1.13

☐ = letter that answers the decoded question in code 1.12

WORD 2

- ☐ = letter that answers the decoded question in code 1.15
- ☐ = letter that answers the decoded question in code 1.11
- ☐ = letter that answers the decoded question in code 1.16
- ☐ = letter that answers the decoded question in code 1.7

WORD 3

- ☐ = first letter of the 10th word of the decoded message in code 1.8
- ☐ = second letter of the decoded message in code 1.2
- ☐ = fourth letter in the third word of the decoded message in code 1.10
- ☐ = final letter of the decoded message in code 1.10

Finally, copy WORD 1 and WORD 2 into the spaces below. But—before you copy WORD 3—apply the instructions from the decoded text in code 1.6.

WORD 1	WORD 2	WORD 3

You should now have a three-word location, which you'll head off to when you turn the page!

< / WRITE THE THREE-WORD LOCATION HERE / >

<MOUNT EVEREST
DORM ROOM>

YOU'VE PASSED THE FIRST SET OF CHALLENGES and made it to the Mount Everest dorm room, where explorer Cruz Coronado spent his first year at Explorer Academy. At the Academy, each room in the student quarters is modeled after natural wonders of the world.

In the library, you honed your code-cracking skills by solving ciphers that involved rearranging letters or words or reading only specific letters or words. In this chapter, the technique gets more advanced: You'll even tackle codes that require changing every letter in a sentence! The codes are hidden all throughout this room—and it looks like the first one is under the pillow. Ready, explorer? Gear up and let's get climbing!

TEMPERATURES AT THE SUMMIT OF MOUNT EVEREST— EARTH'S HIGHEST MOUNTAIN—RANGE FROM AN AVERAGE OF MINUS 4°F (-20°C) TO MINUS 31°F (-35°C).

Mount Everest Dorm Room

/ CODE 2.1 /

A CIPHER IS ANY KIND OF SECRET or disguised way of writing. There are many different kinds of cipher, including the Caesar cipher. To create a Caesar cipher, you shift each letter up or down the alphabet by a fixed number of positions. In the simplest possible Caesar cipher, A becomes B, B becomes C, and so on until you reach the end of the alphabet and Y becomes Z, and Z becomes A.

You can write this out as a table, where the top row is the letter you start with, and the letter below is what it becomes after you have applied the cipher:

A	B	C	D	E	F	G	H	I	J	K	L	M
B	C	D	E	F	G	H	I	J	K	L	M	N

N	O	P	Q	R	S	T	U	V	W	X	Y	Z
O	P	Q	R	S	T	U	V	W	X	Y	Z	A

To decode a message that has been disguised using the cipher, you use the table in reverse, changing from a letter in the bottom row to a letter in the top row. For example, to decode the text XFMM EPOF, you would change X to W, change F to E, and so on until you have revealed "WELL DONE."

Now try decoding the following text:

JU DBO UBLF UXP NPOUIT UP DMJNC NPVOU
FWFSFTU!

< / WRITE THE DECODED MESSAGE HERE / >

> **NOW THAT YOU'VE CRACKED YOUR FIRST CAESAR CIPHER,** this next code should be much easier. Look, there's the next code on the windowsill!

The cipher you just found is another Caesar cipher, but instead of shifting forward through the alphabet by one letter, this time the coding will shift each letter in the opposite direction: A will become Z, B will become A, C will become B, and so on.

To help understand this code, you can create a table to show how each letter changes. Only some of the letters have been written in this time, so can you start by completing the table? The top rows show the original letter, and the bottom rows show what it will become once it has been encoded using the Caesar cipher.

A	B	C	D	E	F	G	H	I	J	K	L	M
Z	A	B	C							J	K	L

N	O	P	Q	R	S	T	U	V	W	X	Y	Z
M	N	O								W	X	Y

CODE 2.2

Use this new Caesar code to decode the following message:

SGD XNTMFDRS ODQRNM SN BKHLA LNTMS
DUDQDRS VZR SGHQSDDM-XDZQ-NKC INQCZM
QNLDQN

< / WRITE THE DECODED MESSAGE HERE / >

{ HUBBARD'S HINT } REMEMBER THAT, WHEN DECODING, YOU SHOULD CONVERT EACH LETTER BY FINDING IT IN THE BOTTOM ROW FIRST AND THEN CHANGING IT TO THE CORRESPONDING LETTER IN THE TOP ROW.

WHAT'S THAT TAPED UNDER CRUZ'S DESK? You've found the last Caesar cipher, and it's the toughest. In this one, the letters have all been encoded by shifting forward by an unknown number of letters in the alphabet. You don't know exactly how many letters forward they've been shifted, only that it is a shift of 10 letters or less.

CODE 2.3

Can you crack the code?

YMJ TQIJXY UJWXTS YT HQNRG RTZSY JAJWJXY
BFX JNLMYD-DJFW-TQI DZNHMNWT RNZWF

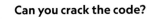

< / WRITE THE HIDDEN QUESTION HERE / >

{ HUBBARD'S HINT } IF YOU'RE STUCK, TRY STARTING WITH THE ASSUMPTION THAT THE CODE HAD A SHIFT OF ONE LETTER FOR THE FIRST WORD. IF THAT DOESN'T MAKE SENSE, TRY A SHIFT OF TWO LETTERS, AND SO ON. YOU CAN ALSO USE THIS TABLE TO HELP TRY OUT DIFFERENT CODES. USE A PENCIL SO YOU CAN ERASE ANY GUESSES THAT TURN OUT TO BE WRONG!

A	B	C	D	E	F	G	H	I	J	K	L	M

N	O	P	Q	R	S	T	U	V	W	X	Y	Z

IT'S TIME FOR A DIFFERENT TYPE OF CIPHER: Explorers, meet the keyed Caesar cipher! Keyed Caesar ciphers also involve swapping one letter for another. But what makes these ciphers super sneaky is that the key to solving them is a **secret code** phrase that only you and your friends know.

To create this cipher, you start by deciding what your **code phrase** is going to be. You then draw out a table, like the ones you've seen already, and you write your code phrase across the top row of it, ignoring any spaces and punctuation. For example, if your code phrase is "I LOVE CATS" then you would start like this:

I	L	O	V	E	C	A	T	S					

Next, you write the rest of the alphabet in order into the top row after the phrase, being careful not to repeat any letters. For example, you already have an A and a C, so the next two letters you write in would be B and D. Once you've done this for "I LOVE CATS," your table looks like this:

I	L	O	V	E	C	A	T	S	B	D	F	G

H	J	K	M	N	P	Q	R	U	W	X	Y	Z

And then, finally, you write in the alphabet in the second row, from A to Z, so your secret encoding table now looks like this:

I	L	O	V	E	C	A	T	S	B	D	F	G
A	B	C	D	E	F	G	H	I	J	K	L	M

H	J	K	M	N	P	Q	R	U	W	X	Y	Z
N	O	P	Q	R	S	T	U	V	W	X	Y	Z

> TO ENCODE A MESSAGE USING THIS CIPHER, you swap each letter in the top row for the corresponding letter in the bottom row. For example, "DOG" would become KCM. If you instead want to decode a message, then you just use the table in reverse, so you replace each letter in the bottom row with its corresponding letter in the top row.

CODE 2.4

Using "I LOVE CATS" as your code phrase, decode this message:

QAFE UVBE HNE WCUBK

< / WRITE THE DECODED MESSAGE HERE / >

Now that you've met the keyed Caesar cipher, it's time to create your own using a different code phrase. This time the code phrase is "MOUNT EVEREST." Unlike "I LOVE CATS," this includes some repeated letters, so to use it you will need to remove not just the space but also any repeated letters, so it looks like this: MOUNTEVRS.

CODE 2.5

Complete the table below and then use it to decode this message:

ABCDE FGFHFIE LHBIIFI EPF KBHMFH KFEWFFD LPQDJ JDM DFUJT

M	O	U	N	T	E	V	R	S				

< / WRITE THE DECODED MESSAGE HERE / >

▷ **EXCELLENT WORK SO FAR.** You are becoming a cipher-cracking master! You can spot the next code on a piece of paper peeking out of a book.

The cipher on this paper is called an Atbash cipher. Despite its unusual name, it is a simple cipher: It involves reversing the entire alphabet. This means that an A becomes a Z, a B becomes a Y, and so on. You can convert letters using the following table:

A	B	C	D	E	F	G	H	I	J	K	L	M
Z	Y	X	W	V	U	T	S	R	Q	P	O	N

N	O	P	Q	R	S	T	U	V	W	X	Y	Z
M	L	K	J	I	H	G	F	E	D	C	B	A

CODE 2.6

The paper has two codes on it. Using the Atbash cipher, decode the first message:

NLFMG VEVIVHG RH PMLDM ZH HZTZINZGSZ RM GSV MVKZOR OZMTFZTV

< / WRITE THE DECODED MESSAGE HERE / >

YOU CAN MAKE THE ATBASH CIPHER EVEN TRICKIER:

As well as reversing the letters of the alphabet, you can also reverse the *order* of the letters within each word.

For example, you could reverse the order of the letters in "CLEVER CODE" to make REVELC EDOC. If you then also applied the Atbash cipher, you would further change REVELC EDOC to IVEVOX VWLX.

To then decode IVEVOX VWLX, you would simply reverse the process: Apply the Atbash cipher again, to get REVELC EDOC, and reverse the letters again, to get back to "CLEVER CODE."

CODE 2.7

Now try decoding the second secret message, which has had both the Atbash cipher applied *and* the order of its letters reversed:

GMFLN GHVIVEV HR WVOOZX ZNTMFOLNLSX MR VSG MZGVYRG VTZFTMZO

< / WRITE THE DECODED MESSAGE HERE / >

WHEW! Those letter-substitution ciphers were pretty challenging, explorer!

This next cipher works differently. It's known as a rail fence cipher because words are written across "rails" of an imaginary fence, moving downward from the top rail and then back upward after reaching the bottom rail. Your message is then written downward and then upward over and over again until the whole message is written out. You can vary the number of rails as you wish, so to decode this type of cipher, you need to know the numbers of rails.

To encode a message, you start by drawing out a table with as many rows as there are rails and as many columns as there are letters in the message. For example, for a message with 10 letters you want to spread out over three rails, you would draw out a table with 10 columns and three rows. Then draw a zigzag line that bounces up and down the table, starting from the top left. It should go up or down one row per column, changing direction each time it reaches the top or bottom of the table, like this:

Now write the letters of the message you want to encode along the line, ignoring spaces but leaving in your punctuation. For example, if the message is "HOW ARE YOU?" you would write:

Now comes the fun part! To extract your encoded message, you read across each row in turn, writing down the letters in the order you come across them. In this example, your message therefore becomes HRUOAEO?WY. This is made up of HRU from the first row, OAEO? from the second row, and finally WY from the third row.

CODE 2.8

Ready to jump in? First, let's try encoding a short message, using a rail fence cipher with three rails. The message is "BEWARE OF SPIES." Use this blank table to work out how this would appear when encoded.

Now write out your encoded message:

{ HUBBARD'S HINT } IF YOU'RE CORRECT, YOU SHOULD HAVE THE LETTER SEQUENCE BRS AT THE START OF YOUR MESSAGE, AND WOI AT THE END.

You spy an odd-looking math problem on a piece of graph paper. Hang on, that's your next code! Now that you're familiar with the rail fence cipher, you're ready to decode the secret message. This time you're going to use a four-rail code. This works in exactly the same way as before, except that you need four rows in your table.

Can you decode this secret message?

ETUØIVSIOTØFHGEESB2ØETHRA9E

Use the following four-row table to help you:

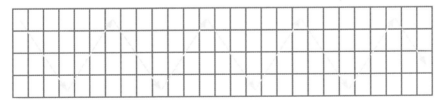

< / WRITE THE DECODED MESSAGE HERE / >

SUDDENLY YOU NOTICE AN ODD FLASHING coming from a computer across the room. It looks like Emmett, Cruz's roommate, was working on something ... no wait, it's the next code! This one uses an even bigger grid ... plus numbers. This code is what's known as a Polybius square, after the ancient Greek historian who was first recorded as using it. A Polybius square looks like this:

	1	2	3	4	5
1	A	B	C	D	E
2	F	G	H	I/J	K
3	L	M	N	O	P
4	Q	R	S	T	U
5	V	W	X	Y	Z

Each letter is assigned a two-digit number based on its position in the grid, using the row number as the first digit and the column number as the second digit. (Remember that rows run from left to right and columns run from top to bottom.) This means, for example, that "DOG" would become 14 34 22, because D is in the 1 row and 4 column, O is in the 3 row and 4 column, and G is in the 2 row and 2 column.

The table is 5 x 5, which means there is only space for 25 letters (since 5 x 5 = 25), so I and J share a square and are both encoded as 24. This means that if you come across 24 when decoding a message, you need to use your judgment to decide whether it should be decoded as an I or a J.

CODE 2.9

Can you *encode* the following message using the Polybius square? Some of the encoded numbers are given for you, so you can check you are correct as you go:

DANGER   IS   ALL   AROUND

< / WRITE THE ENCODED MESSAGE HERE / >

14 ___ ___ ___ 15 ___   ___ ___   ___ ___   31 ___ 34 ___ ___

CODE 2.10

Now can you use the Polybius square to decode the answer to the following question:

Who were the first two people to ascend to the peak of Mount Everest?

44 15 33 55 24 33 22   33 34 42 22 11 54
11 33 14   15 14 32 45 33 14   23 24 31 31 11 42 54

< / WRITE THE DECODED MESSAGE HERE / >

GEOLOGISTS
BELIEVE A
7.8-MAGNITUDE
EARTHQUAKE
IN 2015 MAY HAVE CHANGED
THE HEIGHT OF MOUNT
EVEREST BY SEVERAL
CENTIMETERS.

{ HUBBARD'S HINT }
IN CODE 2.10, 24 DECODES TO THE LETTER I.

THE NEXT CODE IS EVEN MORE CHALLENGING. The Polybius square changes each letter into a number. Codes like this are easy to break with computer analysis, so for a supersecret code, it would be better to create a more complex version of the Polybius.

In this new code, there are four possible numbers for each letter. This happens because there are two digits for each row and column, like this:

	1/6	2/7	3/8	4/9	5/0
1/6	A	B	C	D	E
2/7	F	G	H	I/J	K
3/8	L	M	N	O	P
4/9	Q	R	S	T	U
5/0	V	W	X	Y	Z

Now you can write each letter in four different ways. For example, D could be written as 14, 19, 64, or 69. All of them would decode to D.

You can also write numbers using this code, just to make things even trickier. One way to do this is to add numbers to some squares, just as I and J already share a square. You can do that by adding the digits 1 to 9 and Ø to the first 10 squares that don't contain a vowel, like this:

	1/6	2/7	3/8	4/9	5/0
1/6	A	B/1	C/2	D/3	E
2/7	F/4	G/5	H/6	I/J	K/7
3/8	L/8	M/9	N/Ø	O	P
4/9	Q	R	S	T	U
5/0	V	W	X	Y	Z

TO TELL THE DIFFERENCE BETWEEN A NUMBER AND A WORD when decoding a message, look for the vowels. Because all regular English words contain either a vowel or a Y, if there isn't one of these in the encoded word, then you can be pretty sure that you should decode it as a number instead.

For example, "BAD" could be encoded as 17 66 19. Here, the 66 automatically tells you that the 17 and 19 can't represent digits because 66 can't be a digit—so it must instead decode to the word "BAD" and not to a number.

As an example of encoding a number, you might write "I AM 10 YEARS OLD" as 29 61 87   12 83   54 60 66 42 48   89 31 19. When you then came to decode it, the 12 83 could either read as "BN," which you know is not a word, or as "10," which makes much more sense—so you know it is a number.

CODE 2.11

Try decoding this message, which includes both letters and numbers. Can you figure out what it says?

44 23 60   26 74 92 43 49   61 43 63 10 88 99
84 26   60 51 15 42 65 43 94   52 66 48   24 33
62 82 22 19

< / WRITE THE DECODED MESSAGE HERE / >

MOUNT
EVEREST
IS ABOUT
60 MILLION
YEARS OLD.

GOOD JOB, EXPLORER! But it looks like Emmett's computer holds more challenges for you. While you were in the library, you used a code where the vowels all changed. In that code, an A became an E, an E became an I, an I became an O, an O became a U, and a U became an A. This made the encoded messages harder to read, but you could still figure them out if you knew the trick.

For a code that's much harder to crack, you can use the same vowel-shift code but also encode the consonants, too. You can use a Caesar shift forward of one that applies only to the consonants; because the vowels are already encoded, you skip them. This means that B becomes C, C becomes D, but then D becomes F (skipping E).

Writing this in a table, with the original letters in the top rows and the encoded letters in the bottom rows, your new code works like this:

A	B	C	D	E	F	G	H	I	J	K	L	M
E	C	D	F	I	G	H	J	O	K	L	M	N

N	O	P	Q	R	S	T	U	V	W	X	Y	Z
P	U	Q	R	S	T	V	A	W	X	Y	Z	B

CODE 2.12

Using this new code, can you decode the following question?

XJEV FU NUAPV IWISITV EPF E KANCU KIV JEWI OP DUNNUP?

< / WRITE THE DECODED QUESTION HERE / >

▶ **THIS CODE CAN WORK WITH DIFFERENT SIZES OF SHIFT,** just as with regular Caesar shifts. For example, with a shift of two forward, B would become D, C would become F, and so on. The vowels could also be shifted two forward, so that A would become I (instead of E, as it did when it was shifted forward one vowel), E would become O (instead of I), and so on.

CODE 2.13

Can you complete this table so that this code now works a shift forward of two consonants and a shift of two vowels? Some letters are already given, to help you.

A	B	C	D	E	F	G	H	I	J	K	L	M
I	D	F		O		J					N	

N	O	P	Q	R	S	T	U	V	W	X	Y	Z
		R					E			Z	B	C

Use your completed table to decode the following answer to the coded question on the previous page:

WKOUT YUQG VROOG IQG WIMO-AHH VROOG ITO VAPOWUPOV WKO VIPO!

< / WRITE THE DECODED ANSWER HERE / >

THE HIGHEST RECORDED **WIND SPEED** AT MOUNT EVEREST'S SUMMIT WAS **175 MILES** AN HOUR (282 KM/H).

CONGRATULATIONS, EXPLORER–

YOU'VE FOUND THE FINAL CODE AND REACHED THE SUMMIT!
All you need to do to plant your flag on this chapter of codes
is to crack this last one. Are you ready? Remember: Even master codebreakers can't crack every code! If you don't have all the answers you need,
you can always check the solutions at the back of the book.

CODE 2.14

For this puzzle, you will use the solution to some of the
puzzles you have solved already to find where you should
go next. You will also use some of your new code-cracking
skills. Once you have figured it out, turn the page to
continue your adventure!

The next location is described by a two-word phrase:

WORD 1

STEP ONE: Start with 22 43 51.

STEP TWO: Decode these three numbers to letters using the
Polybius square.

STEP THREE: Then decode those letters using the Atbash cipher.

☐ ☐ ☐ = **three resulting letters from the steps above**

WORD 2

☐ = first letter of the Tibetan name of Mount Everest

☐ = second letter of the Nepali name of Mount Everest

☐ = second letter of the English name of the mountain that is about 29,000 feet (8,839 m) high

☐ = first letter of the first name of the explorer Hillary, who climbed Everest in 1953

FINAL STEP

Copy WORD 1 and WORD 2 into the spaces below, to reveal where you're going next:

☐☐☐☐☐☐☐☐☐ ☐☐☐☐☐☐☐☐☐

WORD 1   WORD 2

< / WRITE THE TWO—WORD LOCATION HERE / >

‹THE CAVE›

Welcome to the
Computer Animated Virtual Experience!

You'll do all of your training missions here in the CAVE. We use the latest technology to combine holographic imagery, thermal radiation sensory technology, three-dimensional printing, and climate control to simulate real-life challenges you'll encounter as an explorer. The goal is to teach you how to handle tricky situations in here so you can confidently face them out in the real elements.

When you're in the CAVE, you'll need to communicate with your fellow explorers. And you'll need to adjust your communication techniques—noises, notes, hand signals, and more—depending on the environment you're in and who you're with.

Get ready to master lots of different communication codes—and how to crack them. We'll start with Morse code, as shown in the chart to the right.

MORSE CODE CHART

A	.-	N	-.
B	-...	O	---
C	-.-.	P	.--.
D	-..	Q	--.-
E	.	R	.-.
F	..-.	S	...
G	--.	T	-
H	....	U	..-
I	..	V	...-
J	.---	W	.--
K	-.-	X	-..-
L	.-..	Y	-.--
M	--	Z	--..

/ CODE 3.1 /

Morse code represents letters using sounds or flashes of light of two different lengths. Short sounds or flashes are called dots, and long sounds or flashes are called dashes. This also makes Morse code easy to write down, since you can write the dots as a period . and the dashes as a dash symbol -, as shown in the chart on the opposite page.

An A in Morse code is represented by a dot and a dash. So, if you're communicating with sounds, you would send a short sound followed by a long sound. Or, if you're using a flashlight, it would be a short flash followed by a long flash. Be sure to pause before starting the next letter, so the message recipient knows it's a new letter.

See if you can decipher this written Morse code message. Hint: It's your mission in the CAVE!

. -..- .-. .-.. --- .-. .

< / WRITE THE MESSAGE HERE / >

MORSE CODE WAS ONCE USED TO

send short messages via telegraph machines, which allowed people to communicate quickly over long distances in the days before the telephone was invented. Operators would send and receive audible clicks using a simple machine.

In your CAVE exploration simulation, you find yourself on a remote ship in the Arctic. What secrets await? Use your Morse code knowledge to solve the following codes.

MORSE CODE CHART

A	.-	N	-.
B	-...	O	---
C	-.-.	P	.--.
D	-..	Q	--.-
E	.	R	.-.
F	..-.	S	...
G	--.	T	-
H	....	U	..-
I	..	V	...-
J	.---	W	.--
K	-.-	X	-..-
L	.-..	Y	-.--
M	--	Z	--..

CODE 3.2

Decode the following message, which consists of sounds of different lengths, and see if you too can make sense of an audible Morse code message. The longer sounds (clickety, bleep, and dash) are dashes, and the shorter sounds (click, blip, and dot) are dots. A slash is used to represent a pause between letters, and each set of sounds represents a different word in the phrase.

Click clickety

Bleep / blip / blip bleep blip blip / blip / bleep bleep blip / blip bleep blip / blip bleep / blip bleep bleep blip / blip blip blip blip

Dash dash / dot / dot dot dot / dot dot dot / dot dash / dash dash dot / dot

< / WRITE THE PHRASE HERE / >

MORSE CODE CAN BE USED TO SEND secret messages by finding crafty ways to hide it.

You've received the following message with the words "dash" and "dot" hidden inside it, including some that are sneakily concealed. For example, "veran**da sh**ade" hides a "dash" in the first line of the note below.

CODE 3.3

Every sentence in this seemingly strange note contains one letter of the solution. Can you find the hidden dots and dashes and decode the Morse code message? It will tell you the name of the Explorer Academy student the curious communiqué was intended for.

Don't tell me; you're sitting under the veranda shade, counting the dots on the cloth and waiting to dash off to Orlando this weekend. I know you're sick of having to cook and clean and do the laundry, and a trip to Florida should be a good antidote to your boredom. If you haven't gone shopping yet, I think you should ditch those boring old avocado tops you always wear for a pair of funky, polka-dot panda shorts. You would look more dashing, beyond a shadow of a doubt, and other people would have to do their best not to stare—which is always amusing!

< / WRITE THE HIDDEN WORD HERE / >

{ HUBBARD'S HINT } IF YOU GET STUCK, TRY LOOKING OUT FOR WORDS THAT END IN *D, DO,* OR *DA*, AS THESE ARE OFTEN THE START OF A DOT OR A DASH. THERE ARE 14 DOTS AND DASHES TO FIND.

SEMAPHORE IS ANOTHER WAY to send visual messages. It is a time-tested communication system that involves holding two flags and positioning your arms in certain ways to indicate different letters. Semaphore was once used by sailors at sea, to communicate with people on other ships who were too far away to hear them. Check out the semaphore alphabet here:

So, to communicate the word "HELLO," you'd hold flags in the following positions with your arms, holding each pose briefly before moving on to the next:

Brrr, recruit. Do you feel the chill? The wind has picked up, and it's too loud to hear anything! It's time to use your trusty semaphore skills.

CODE 3.4

Let's see if you can decode the following semaphore message. What is it telling you to do? (Hint: Spaces between words are represented by gaps between people.)

< / WRITE THE MESSAGE HERE / >

PHEW, YOU'RE FINALLY OUT OF THE COLD and in the ship's operating room. But why are there so many clocks? Semaphore traditionally uses flags, but you don't actually need the flags: You just need some way to point in two directions at once, such as the face of a clock.

The minute and hour hands of a clock can represent all the letters of the semaphore alphabet, just as if they were the arms of a person. For example, the clock to the right, showing 7:30, represents the letter A because the hands of the clock are in roughly the same position as the arms of someone making the letter A in flag semaphore. (Flip back a page to take another look at the semaphore alphabet.)

CODE 3.5

This room is full of clocks ... and codes! Using the semaphore alphabet on the previous page, can you decode the message that has been hidden in these clock faces?

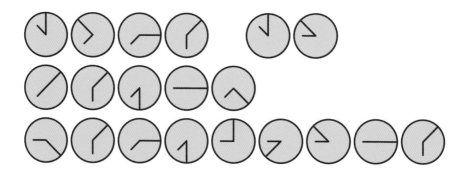

< / WRITE THE MESSAGE HERE / >

IN ADDITION TO THE CLOCKS, you notice lots of similar paintings ... what could they mean? Well, semaphore can be hidden in even sneakier ways than by using clock faces. This can make your secret message even stronger. For example: This might *look* like abstract art, but if you examine the light blue

shape inside each blue rectangle, you'll see that it consists of two lines that run from the center of the shape to the edge of the rectangle—just like the hands on a clock! The pattern to the left therefore represents A, B, and C in semaphore. Use the semaphore table on page 50 to check this for yourself.

CODE 3.6

Now use your semaphore skills to decode the following message. (The empty rectangle represents a space.)

< / WRITE THE MESSAGE HERE / >

SEMAPHORE USES FLAGS TO SEND MESSAGES, but it doesn't matter what the flags actually look like: They are just large objects that are easy to hold, move, and see from a distance. Up next is a code where the flags *do* matter.

Take a look at these flags of different countries around the world:

AFGHANISTAN	ANDORRA	ARGENTINA	AUSTRALIA	AUSTRIA	BANGLADESH	BELGIUM	BOLIVIA
BRAZIL	BULGARIA	CANADA	CHILE	CHINA	CONGO	COSTA RICA	CUBA
DENMARK	DJIBOUTI	ECUADOR	EGYPT	ERITEA	ESTONIA	FRANCE	GERMANY
GREECE	GUATEMALA	HAITI	HUNGARY	ICELAND	INDIA	INDONESIA	IRAQ
IRELAND	ISRAEL	ITALY	JAPAN	KENYA	LAOS	LIBERIA	LITHUANIA
MADAGASCAR	MALTA	MEXICO	MOROCCO	MYANMAR	NETHERLANDS	NORWAY	OMAN
PAKISTAN	PERU	PORTUGAL	RUSSIA	SOUTH AFRICA	SPAIN	SRI LANKA	SUDAN
SWEDEN	TANZANIA	THAILAND	TURKEY	UKRAINE	UNITED KINGDOM	VIETNAM	ZIMBABWE

AS YOU WANDER OUT OF THE OPERATION ROOM

and down the ship's hall, you see flags in all kinds of different colors and designs. But did you know these pennants of national pride can be used to hide a code? Yep: You can use each flag to represent the first letter of the country it belongs to. For example, the French flag would represent the letter F, the Argentine flag would represent the letter A, and so on. Multiple flags can then be used to spell out words.

CODE 3.7

Identify the flags below to decode a secret message and learn a fun fact about flags.

< / WRITE THE MESSAGE HERE / >

READY TO MAKE YOUR FLAG DECODING TWICE AS CHALLENGING? Check out the U.S. state flags on the opposite wall.

 ALABAMA ALASKA ARIZONA ARKANSAS CALIFORNIA COLORADO

 CONNECTICUT DELAWARE DISTRICT OF COLUMBIA FLORIDA GEORGIA HAWAII

 IDAHO ILLINOIS INDIANA IOWA KANSAS KENTUCKY

LOUISIANA MISSOURI MARYLAND MASSACHUSETTS MICHIGAN MINNESOTA

MISSISSIPPI MISSOURI MONTANA NEBRASKA NEVADA NEW HAMPSHIRE

 NEW JERSEY NEW MEXICO NEW YORK NORTH CAROLINA NORTH DAKOTA OHIO

 OKLAHOMA OREGON PENNSYLVANIA RHODE ISLAND SOUTH CAROLINA SOUTH DAKOTA

 TENNESSEE TEXAS UTAH VERMONT VIRGINIA WASHINGTON

 WEST VIRGINIA WISCONSIN WYOMING

You can use these to make a flag-based code, too. But instead of using the first letter of the state, you can use its standard two-letter U.S. postal code abbreviation. For example, the flag of Maine would represent ME. This means that each flag represents two letters, not one.

Alabama	AL	Kentucky	KY	North Dakota	ND
Alaska	AK	Louisiana	LA	Ohio	OH
Arizona	AZ	Maine	ME	Oklahoma	OK
Arkansas	AR	Maryland	MD	Oregon	OR
California	CA	Massachusetts	MA	Pennsylvania	PA
Colorado	CO	Michigan	MI	Rhode Island	RI
Connecticut	CT	Minnesota	MN	South Carolina	SC
Delaware	DE	Mississippi	MS	South Dakota	SD
District of Columbia	DC	Missouri	MO	Tennessee	TN
Florida	FL	Montana	MT	Texas	TX
Georgia	GA	Nebraska	NE	Utah	UT
Hawaii	HI	Nevada	NV	Vermont	VT
Idaho	ID	New Hampshire	NH	Virginia	VA
Illinois	IL	New Jersey	NJ	Washington	WA
Indiana	IN	New Mexico	NM	West Virginia	WV
Iowa	IA	New York	NY	Wisconsin	WI
Kansas	KS	North Carolina	NC	Wyoming	WY

CODE 3.8

The two-letter postal codes for the states represented by the flags below spell out a short phrase. Can you decode the message to find out where you are right now?

< / WRITE YOUR MESSAGE HERE / >

MORSE CODE AND SEMAPHORE ARE VERY WELL-KNOWN

KNOWN methods of communication, so if you are trying to send a super-secret message, you might want to make up your own system of signals instead. That way, no one else will know your code, so it will be much harder for someone to crack your transmissions.

At the Academy, some of the students have developed a system of hand signals to secretly communicate with each other. Hand signals are great, because you don't need any tools like pens, paper, lights, flags, or anything else that might give you away ... or that could be discovered later!

A secret hand code should use only very small movements. (If you wave your hands around in the air, you're sure to be noticed!) The Academy hand code system works by using one or more finger taps of the same hand. It doesn't matter which hand you use.

Beginning from your thumb and then working out to your little finger, each finger represents a different group of letters: Your thumb is A to E, your index finger is F to J, your middle finger is K to O, your ring finger is P to T, and your little finger is U to Z.

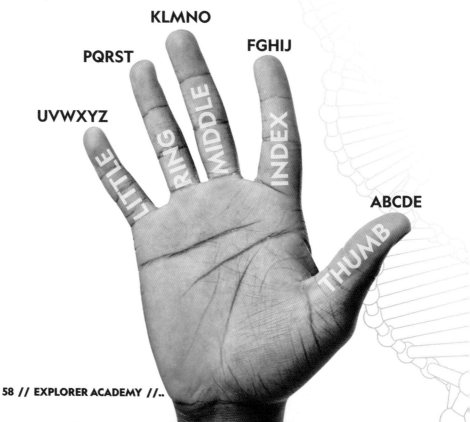

YOU TAP A FINGER ONCE if you want the first letter in a group, or twice for the second letter, three times for the third letter and so on. To send "HELLO," for example, you'd tap your index finger three times, your thumb five times, your middle finger twice, then a pause, then twice again, then another pause and five more taps with your middle finger. To indicate you are starting a new word, you could take a longer pause, move your hand slightly, or change hands.

CODE 3.9

Out of the corner of your eye you notice Bryndis, one of Cruz's friends, looking at you as she taps her fingers on a table underneath the state flags. Could she be sending you a secret warning? Use the information you've been given about hand signals to decipher it. A new line is used for each word.

RING FINGER: 5 taps; INDEX FINGER: 3 taps; THUMB: 5 taps

RING FINGER: 4 taps; RING FINGER: 1 tap; LITTLE FINGER: 5 taps

INDEX FINGER: 4 taps; RING FINGER: 4 taps

MIDDLE FINGER: 4 taps; THUMB: 5 taps; THUMB: 1 tap; RING FINGER: 3 taps

< / WRITE THE WARNING HERE / >

WITH THE WARNING IN MIND, you race back to the safety of your cabin. There you see a pamphlet on the International Radiotelephony Spelling Alphabet! That's a bit of a mouthful, so it's usually just called the NATO alphabet.

The NATO alphabet is used by pilots, police, the military, and others who need to spell names out clearly. It's used over radio communications, where it can be hard to hear the difference between letters like B and D or M and N. You may have heard it in movies or had someone use it to spell something out to you over the phone.

The alphabet represents each individual letter with a word:

A	Alfa (or alpha)	N	November
B	Bravo	O	Oscar
C	Charlie	P	Papa
D	Delta	Q	Quebec
E	Echo	R	Romeo
F	Foxtrot	S	Sierra
G	Golf	T	Tango
H	Hotel	U	Uniform
I	India	V	Victor
J	Juliet	W	Whiskey
K	Kilo	X	X-ray
L	Lima	Y	Yankee
M	Mike	Z	Zulu

YOU CAN USE THE NATO ALPHABET TO HIDE A SECRET MESSAGE by placing its words into an otherwise unimportant piece of text. An old magazine has been left on the floor—could it hold your last clue?

CODE 3.10

Read the following magazine blurb carefully and extract the words of the NATO alphabet, which spell out a secret congratulatory message. You'll need to insert a space after the fourth letter.

November 2017
A Passage to India, adapted for the stage by director/playwright Charlie Lopez, is a visually stunning, emotionally charged theatrical hit. Lopez's script, although it contains a strong echo of Forster's original prose, gives the dialogue a modern twist, and is in equal parts humorous and heart-wrenching. In terms of the cast, lead actress Juliet Tarskaya is a standout as Mrs. Moore. Many have doubted whether Tarskaya would be able to translate her on-screen presence to the stage, but the Oscar nominee gives everything to this role, and is sure to silence the critics. Bravo!

< / WRITE THE MESSAGE HERE / >

{ HUBBARD'S HINT } IF YOU GET STUCK, MAKE SURE YOU'VE READ EVERYTHING IN THE EXTRACT—INCLUDING THE DATE AND THE FINAL ONE-WORD SENTENCE!

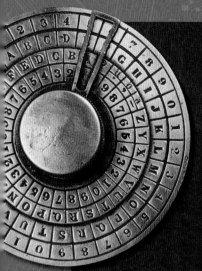

CONGRATULATIONS, EXPLORER—

YOU'VE SURVIVED THE CAVE! All you need to do is step out of the holographic environment and answer a few questions on what you learned inside. Just a reminder that even master codebreakers can't crack every code! If you don't have all the answers you need, you can always check the solutions at the back of the book.

CODE 3.11

 For this puzzle, you will use the solution to some of the codes you have solved already—as well as some of your new code-cracking skills—to find where you should go next. Once you have figured it out, turn the page to journey to the next location of your adventure!

The next location is described by a two-word phrase:

WORD 1

☐ ☐ ☐ = the second word of the secret message in code 3.4

WORD 2

▢ = middle letter of the country with the oldest flag

▢ = the letter represented by the Morse code ..-

▢ = first letter of something that was "double" in an answer to a puzzle

▢ = the letter that starts and ends the decoded message in code 3.1

▢ = the letter represented by 10:10 in semaphore

▢ = three taps of your middle finger

FINAL STEP

Finally, copy WORD 1 and WORD 2 into the spaces below to reveal where you're going next:

WORD 1	WORD 2

You should now have a two-word location, which you'll head off to when you turn the page!

< / WRITE THE TWO-WORD LOCATION HERE / >

<THE SYNTHESIS>

WHOA, RECRUIT: You should not have tried to take that shortcut after leaving the CAVE. According to the security footage, it seems you took a wrong turn and your route was suddenly blocked by a frosted glass door. Before you could realize your mistake, a previously hidden steel panel slid shut behind you, trapping you in a small room. It's now up to you to find your way out so you can make it to the museum, your next stop on the scavenger hunt.

Luckily, you've learned the kinds of skills that any successful codebreaker needs, such as discovering secret access codes! Remember that codes come in all shapes and forms, and not every code you come across will result in a hidden word or message. In some cases, you'll need to reveal a secret sequence of moves, deduce a set of numbers, or even figure out hidden wiring information. Good luck, explorer!

/ CODE 4.1 /

THERE DOESN'T SEEM TO BE ANY WAY to open the steel door from where you are, so you'll have to get creative. See that maintenance panel next to the glass door? Inside, a tangle of wires plus some buttons is visible.

Which one of the buttons is connected to the door mechanism? Perhaps if you press that button you will be able to open the glass door.

DOOR MECHANISM

< / WRITE THE COLOR OF THE BUTTON HERE / >

YOU GOT THE GLASS DOOR OPEN—great work, recruit! But where are you? This was not part of your official scavenger hunt. You've heard rumblings about a secret area on campus called the Synthesis. Could you have stumbled your way into the most classified lab in the world?

Unfortunately, you don't see any exits. The room you are in is mostly bare except for the wall in front of you, which contains two incomplete wiring circuits, along with a pile of disconnected wires. What will happen if you wire up both circuits?

CODE 4.2

Check out the diagram below. Can you draw wires along the dashed lines to join the pairs of matching shapes? The wires can't cross over or touch each other in any way; if they do, that will short-circuit the system.

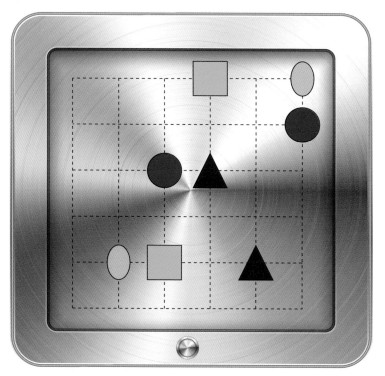

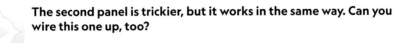

CODE 4.3

The second panel is trickier, but it works in the same way. Can you wire this one up, too?

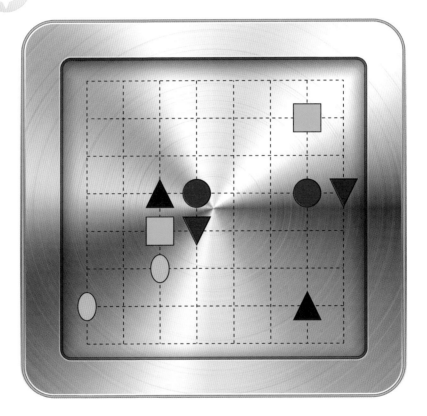

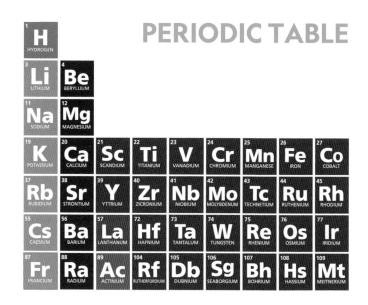

PERIODIC TABLE

¹ H HYDROGEN								
³ Li LITHIUM	⁴ Be BERYLLIUM							
¹¹ Na SODIUM	¹² Mg MAGNESIUM							
¹⁹ K POTASSIUM	²⁰ Ca CALCIUM	²¹ Sc SCANDIUM	²² Ti TITANIUM	²³ V VANADIUM	²⁴ Cr CHROMIUM	²⁵ Mn MANGANESE	²⁶ Fe IRON	²⁷ Co COBALT
³⁷ Rb RUBIDIUM	³⁸ Sr STRONTIUM	³⁹ Y YTTRIUM	⁴⁰ Zr ZICRONIUM	⁴¹ Nb NIOBIUM	⁴² Mo MOLYBDENUM	⁴³ Tc TECHNETIUM	⁴⁴ Ru RUTHENIUM	⁴⁵ Rh RHODIUM
⁵⁵ Cs CAESIUM	⁵⁶ Ba BARIUM	⁵⁷ La LANTHANUM	⁷² Hf HAFNIUM	⁷³ Ta TANTALUM	⁷⁴ W TUNGSTEN	⁷⁵ Re RHENIUM	⁷⁶ Os OSMIUM	⁷⁷ Ir IRIDIUM
⁸⁷ Fr FRANCIUM	⁸⁸ Ra RADIUM	⁸⁹ Ac ACTINIUM	¹⁰⁴ Rf RUTHERFORDIUM	¹⁰⁵ Db DUBNIUM	¹⁰⁶ Sg SEABORGIUM	¹⁰⁷ Bh BOHRIUM	¹⁰⁸ Hs HASSIUM	¹⁰⁹ Mt MEITNERIUM

AS YOU CONNECT THE LAST WIRE, you notice something strange happening to a wall on one side of the room. A portion of it has changed to reveal a hidden door!

You walk over and peer through the door's small window for a closer look. Inside is a laboratory with a copy of the periodic table on the wall.

The periodic table lists the elements that make up everything in the universe, from the air we breathe, to the world we see, to our very own bodies. Each element is identified by its atomic number, which is the number of positively charged particles (protons) in the center (nucleus) of that element's atoms. The periodic table assigns each element an abbreviation (indicated by the letters in the table) and an atomic number. For example, "He" has an atomic number of 2, and "As" has an atomic number of 33.

ATOMS ARE THE BUILDING BLOCKS OF ALL MATTER. AN ELEMENT IS A SUBSTANCE MADE OF JUST ONE KIND OF ATOM.

OF ELEMENTS

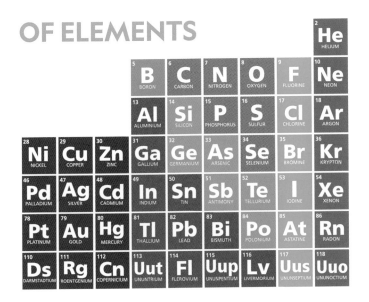

CODE 4.4

On the wall next to the newly revealed door is a computer panel. It starts beeping to attract your attention, then flashes bright red warning text. It is requesting an access password for the laboratory. The panel displays a password hint:

A keyboard with the letters A to Z appears on the panel. What password should you enter?

< / WRITE THE PASSWORD HERE / >

{ HUBBARD'S HINT } WHAT ARE THE ELEMENT ABBREVIATIONS FOR EACH OF THESE NUMBERS? TRY WRITING THEM ALL OUT IN ORDER, ONE AFTER THE OTHER.

▷ **YOU ENTER THE PASSWORD,** and the panel changes from an angry red to a calming green. The panel now requests a numeric access code, displaying a different password hint:

NUMERIC
PASSWORD REQUIRED
HINT: *ATTENTION*

0 1 2 3 4 5 6 7 8 9

CODE 4.5

A number pad with digits from 0 to 9 appears. What numeric access code should you enter?

< / WRITE THE CODE HERE / >

{ HUBBARD'S HINT } SOLVING THE PASSWORD WILL REQUIRE USING THE ABBREVIATIONS OF SIX ELEMENTS. SPLIT UP THE WORD, STARTING WITH "AT" FOR THE FIRST PART.

TO YOUR SURPRISE, the panel is requesting a third and final code! This time it requires a two-digit number. The panel once again displays a hint:

2-DIGIT
PASSWORD REQUIRED
HINT: *CONNECT THESE*

7-6-5-13-31-32-33-51-83-82-81
32-31-13-5-6-7-15-33-51-83-82-81

__ __

0 1 2 3 4 5 6 7 8 9

CODE 4.6

What is the required two-digit number?

< / WRITE THE CODE HERE / >

{ HUBBARD'S HINT } FIND THESE NUMBERS ON THE PERIODIC TABLE AND TRACE A PATH FROM THE FIRST TO THE LAST OF EACH SET OF NUMBERS WITH YOUR FINGER. WHAT DOES EACH PATH LOOK LIKE?

THE DOOR OPENS AND YOU NOW HAVE FULL ACCESS

to the laboratory. Tread carefully, recruit! You head for a door at the end of the room, but it's locked. However, two experiments appear to be in progress, and both are requesting assistance on nearby screens.

The first experiment involves a set of three measuring jars. Two jars are empty, while a third is full to the brim with some type of liquid. It could be dangerous, so you don't want to spill any of it.

The first jar is empty, but it can hold 3 liters. The second is empty, but it can hold 7 liters. The third is full, and it is holding 10 liters.

The screen is requesting that you pour the liquid between the jars so that you end up with exactly 8 liters in jar C. To get exactly 8 liters, you will need to do this mathematically rather than by eyeballing it. **Each time you pour the liquid, you must either fill one jar or empty another—you can't stop in between.** And remember: You can't spill any.

For example, you could pour jar C into jar B. You would then have 7 liters in B and leave 3 liters in C. If you then poured jar B into jar A, you would end up with 3 liters in A, 4 liters in B, and 3 liters in C.

CODE 4.7

Let's use those codebreaking puzzle-solving skills to solve this one.
Can you figure out how to end up with exactly 8 liters in jar C?

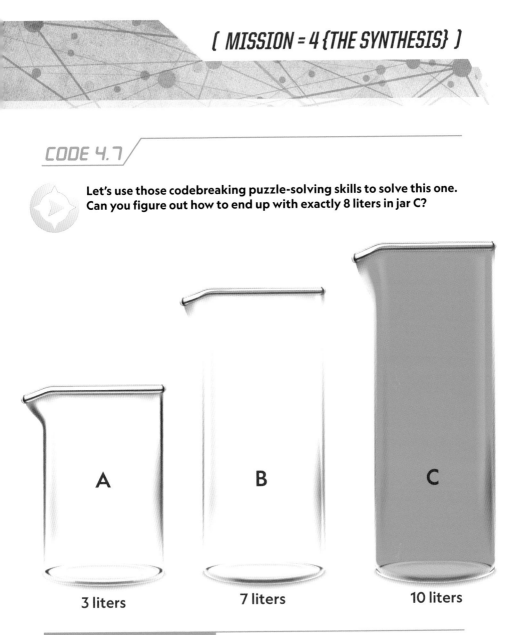

A
3 liters

B
7 liters

C
10 liters

< / WRITE YOUR STEPS HERE / >

HAVING COMPLETED THE FIRST EXPERIMENT, you turn your attention to the second. This experiment features a scale along with six weights. The weights have the following values:

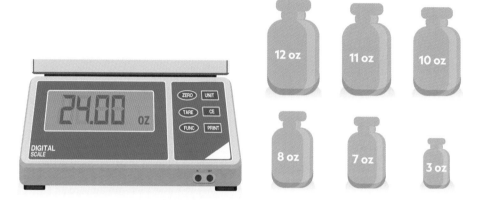

The screen alongside the scale is requesting that you place weights on the scales that add up to a total weight of **24 oz.**

CODE 4.8

Which weights should you place on the scale?

< / WRITE THE WEIGHTS HERE / >

{ HUBBARD'S HINT } YOU'LL NEED TO USE THREE WEIGHTS TO MAKE UP THE TOTAL OF 24 OZ.

CODE 4.9

You place the correct weights on the scale, but the computer then requests three more total weights! Can you figure out how to make each of the following, one at a time, too?

< / WRITE THE WEIGHTS HERE / >

 { HUBBARD'S HINT } FOR 27 OZ, YOU'LL NEED THREE WEIGHTS; FOR 34 OZ, YOU'LL NEED FOUR WEIGHTS; AND FOR 39 OZ, YOU'LL NEED FIVE WEIGHTS. YOU MIGHT ALSO FIND IT EASIER, FOR 34 OZ AND 39 OZ, TO ADD UP ALL THE WEIGHTS AND FIGURE OUT WHICH ONES TO TAKE AWAY FROM THE FULL TOTAL.

AFTER YOU FINISH BOTH EXPERIMENTS, a panel by the door back out of the lab lights up. It is displaying a series of numbers that don't appear to mean anything at first. You soon notice that all the numbers are in the range 1 to 26, which makes you stop and think. What is special about the number 26? In a code, the numbers 1 to 26 could correspond to ... what?

AHA! YOU REALIZE THAT THE NUMBERS 1 to 26 on the door panel probably correspond to the letters of the alphabet, since there are 26 different letters in the English alphabet.

In a letter-to-number code, each letter can be written as a number like this:

A	B	C	D	E	F	G	H	I	J	K	L	M
1	2	3	4	5	6	7	8	9	10	11	12	13

N	O	P	Q	R	S	T	U	V	W	X	Y	Z
14	15	16	17	18	19	20	21	22	23	24	25	26

For example, "THIS WORD" would be written as 20-8-9-19 23-15-18-4.

To convert back from a number to a letter, you find the number in the bottom row of the table and change it to the letter above. This means, for example, that 25-5-19 converts to "YES."

CODE 4.10

The panel is displaying various messages, but the most important message appears to be the one below. What does it say?

12-5-1-22-5   9-14   5-24-1-3-20-12-25
14-9-14-5   13-9-14-21-20-5-19

< / WRITE THE MESSAGE HERE / >

▷ **JUST AS YOU FINISH READING THE MESSAGE,** the panel changes to request a "countdown activation" code. To start the countdown, you must enter the correct message into the panel using its numeric keypad.

COUNTDOWN
ACTIVATION REQUIRED
HINT: *START*

_ _ _ _ _ _ _ _

0 1 2 3 4 5 6 7 8 9

CODE 4.11

Using the code on the previous page, what numbers would you type to enter "START" using the numeric keypad?

< / WRITE THE MESSAGE HERE / >

YOU HAVE SUCCESSFULLY STARTED THE COUNTDOWN.

According to the solution to code 4.10, you will have the chance to leave in exactly nine minutes. Great! As you make your way to the door to wait it out, you spot two old-timey wooden sand timers on a shelf next to the exit, along with some other antique-looking objects. All seem a little out of place in the lab.

▶ **YOU GRAB THE SAND TIMERS OFF THE SHELF** and examine them more closely. Each is labeled with the amount of time it takes for sand to pass through: five minutes for one and seven minutes for the other. And they are not as old-fashioned as they first appeared; each has wires coming out of the bottom that are connected to … the door's control panel!

You suddenly realize the significance of "nine minutes": It's one last clue. You must time exactly nine minutes using these two timers for the doors to actually open at the end of the countdown.

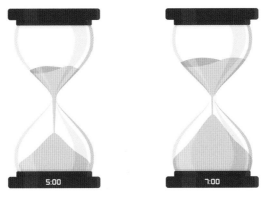

CODE 4.12

There is a mathematical way to do it, by turning them over at just the right moments. Can you figure out how to time exactly nine minutes?

< / WRITE THE STEPS HERE / >

{ HUBBARD'S HINT } WHEN ONE OF THE TIMERS FINISHES, WHAT HAPPENS IF YOU TURN THE OTHER ONE OVER IMMEDIATELY, EVEN IF IT HASN'T YET FINISHED?

YOU DID IT,
EXPLORER–

NINE MINUTES AFTER THE COUNTDOWN BEGAN, the exit door opened and then quickly closed again. Good job!

In this next room, you notice a keypad under a steel sign that reads DOOR RELEASE. Could it be ... ? Yes! This seems to be the way to finally unlock the steel door that will let you return to the correct route.

Searching around the keypad, you find a folded piece of paper that seems to be designed to help someone figure out how to open the door if they do not know the code. It says:

To exit: 10-9-8-16-34-35-34-52-84
10-9-8-16-34-35-34-52-84-85-86

Curious. You suspect you'll be able to use a skill you picked up during your detour ... and you're right! This looks like the panel you used to spell out digits in code 4.6, but when you trace them this time you will end up with letters instead. And yet the keypad is still requiring a two-digit number. Is there some sort of table you can use to convert the two letters you trace into a two-digit number?

CODE 4.13

What two-digit code should you type into the keypad to open the door?

```
2-DIGIT
PASSWORD REQUIRED

_   _

0 1 2 3 4 5 6 7 8 9
```

< / WRITE THE CODE HERE / >

You punch in the solution and double back to find that the steel door has slid open. Finally, you're back on the right track!

{ HUBBARD'S HINT } USE THE PERIODIC TABLE TO CONVERT THE LETTERS INTO A TWO-LETTER ELEMENT SYMBOL. STILL STUCK? WHAT'S THE ATOMIC NUMBER FOR THAT ELEMENT?

‹THE MUSEUM›

YOU'VE FINALLY MADE IT TO THE MUSEUM
after that unexpected detour. Nice work, recruit!

In this location, you'll be cracking visual codes, where pictures are used instead of letters or words. Each code can be found at one of the museum's exhibits.

One type of visual code is the pigpen cipher. It works by laying out all the letters of the alphabet in four grids, like this:

/ CODE 5.1 /

Each letter is then replaced by a picture that looks like the part of the grid it's in, like this:

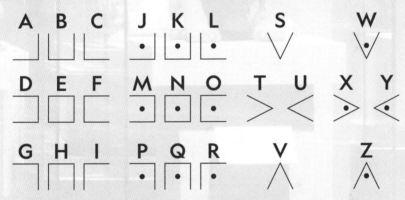

For the pictures with dots inside, it doesn't matter where you draw the dot so long as it's somewhere within the shape for that letter.

Can you decode the following pigpen message?

< / WRITE THE DECODED MESSAGE HERE / >

A BIG ADVANTAGE OF PIGPEN

is that it's easy to remember how the grids are laid out, so you can use it even if you don't have a copy of the code with you. Check out this code at the exhibit on butterfly migrations.

CODE 5.2

 Can you fill in these empty pigpen grids, writing in all the letters from A to Z?

Now, without checking back to the previous page, can you decode this pigpen message? A warning, though: It has had all its spaces removed to make it trickier. It's up to you to figure out where the missing spaces should go!

< / WRITE THE MESSAGE HERE / >

{ HUBBARD'S HINT } IF YOU GET STUCK, CHECK BACK TO THE PREVIOUS TWO PAGES. THERE ARE THREE SPACES MISSING. THE FIRST ONE SHOULD GO AFTER THE FIFTH LETTER.

PIGPEN CAN BE COMBINED with many of the codes you've already encountered in earlier locations, to make it even sneakier.

Your next stop is a display on butterfly tracking methods, like the ones Sailor and Cruz used in the CAVE. You quickly spot some pigpen symbols! In this message, the letters have been changed using the Atbash cipher from page 34. This means that A and Z have been swapped with one another, B and Y have been swapped, C and X have been swapped, and so on.

CODE 5.3

What does this message say? To decode it, first convert the pigpen symbols into letters and then use the Atbash cipher to decode each of the letters.

< / WRITE THE MESSAGE HERE / >

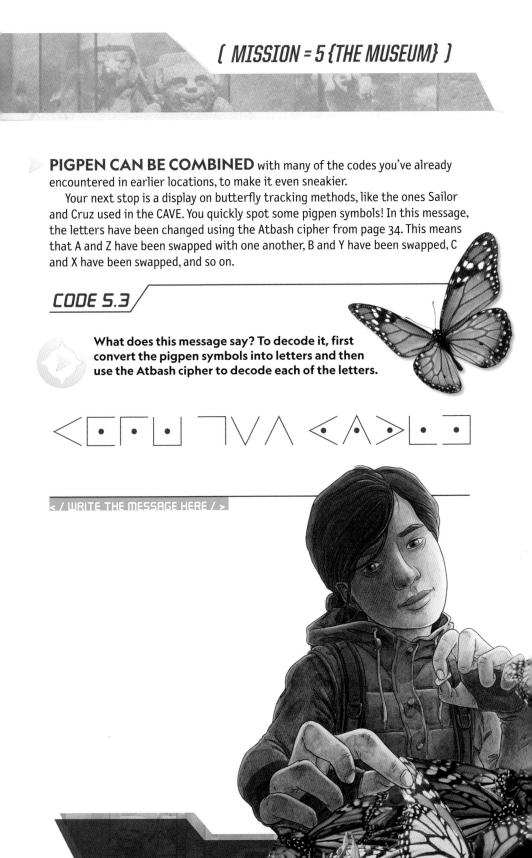

PIGPEN IS A WELL-KNOWN CODE, so to write a really secret message, it might be a good idea to use something different. The best way to do this is to create a code yourself, so that only you and the person you want to communicate with know what it means. This is what Cruz's mom did so she could send him a message that only he could read. Her code was based on spirals. The alphabet for Cruz's mom's spiral cipher looks like this:

AT THE NEXT EXHIBIT, YOU FIND A SCROLL WITH PRETTY SPIRALS.
The differences between the spirals are pretty small, making it hard to crack the code. You have to look carefully to tell the letters apart: Check where each spiral starts and ends to figure out which letter is which!

CODE 5.4

Use Cruz's mom's spiral code to decode this phrase:

< / WRITE THE MESSAGE HERE / >

HOW CREEPY! BUT YOU NEED TO KEEP MOVING ON.

You head to the ancient Egypt hall. Symbols and pictures aren't just reserved for codes: The ancient Egyptians had a complex, picture-based writing system. They carved likenesses of everyday objects into stone to convey concepts, numbers, and speech sounds. We now call these pictures hieroglyphs, and there are thousands of different pictures in this alphabet.

Hieroglyphs can also be used to write numbers, and one way that this can be done is by using hieroglyphic digits. Unlike our 0 to 9 digits, however, Egyptian hieroglyphic digits are based on multiples of 10. They represent 1; 10; 100; 1,000; 10,000; 100,000; or 1,000,000. The Egyptians would then repeat a digit if they wanted to represent more than one of a multiple. So, to write the number 3, the Egyptians would write the hieroglyph for "1" three times. Or to write the number 20, they would use the hieroglyph for "10" two times.

The digits look like this:

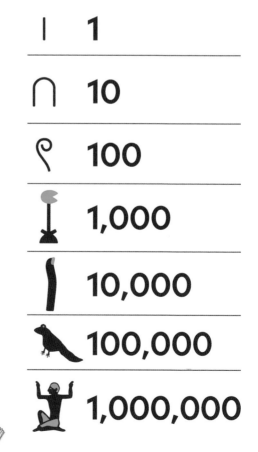

DIFFERENT HIEROGLYPHS CAN BE COMBINED to make any number. You write them close together so it's clear they are all one number. For example, the number 3,412 could be written like this:

CODE 5.5

Wait, some of the hieroglyphs in the exhibit look out of place. Can you decode the following six numbers, each written in hieroglyphs? Once you have figured out the numbers, read the letters beneath them in decreasing numerical order of the hieroglyphs above them, starting from the largest. What word results?

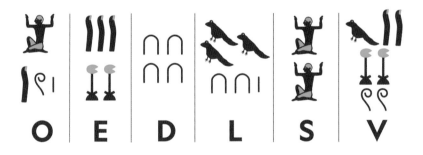

O | E | D | L | S | V

< / WRITE THE WORD HERE / >

O =
E =
D =

L =
S = 2,000,0000
V =

S
___ ___ ___ ___ ___ ___

{ HUBBARD'S HINT } THE SECOND LARGEST NUMBER IS THE ONE ABOVE THE LETTER O, WHICH IS 1,010,101.

GOOD JOB, EXPLORER—NOW HEAD TO THE MAPS
EXHIBIT. So far, you've seen three kinds of visual code in the museum. The symbols that these codes use are pretty obvious, however, so even if someone couldn't read your code, they might well notice the strange symbols and wonder what they mean. So what if you want to hide a message in a picture so nobody would know it was even there?

One way to hide a message is to use a map, like the one on this page. The first letters of the places marked on the map can then be used to spell out a secret message. You just need to know which places you should look at to decode the message.

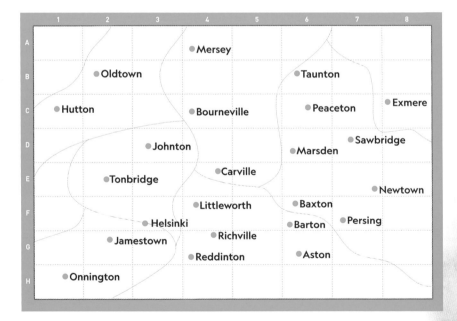

CODE 5.6

To reveal the message hidden on this map, find the place at each of the following coordinates and take its first letter. What message does it spell out?

E7-B2-E2   B6-H1   D7-E4-G6-F4-C8

< / WRITE THE MESSAGE HERE / >

THIS CODE IS TOP SECRET

because it requires two items that can be hidden separately and don't obviously go together. The map without the key is of no use, and the key without the map is of no help, either. This makes it harder for enemy spies to steal your message!

THERE ARE EVEN MORE WAYS TO HIDE A MESSAGE ON A MAP.

If you follow a path from place to place, drawing your route on a map, you could trace out the shape of letters and numbers. The only downside with this method is that you need to visit a lot of places and draw a lot of lines to write even just a short secret message!

Try it with the towns below and see how it works.

	1	2	3	4	5	6	7	8
A				Mersey				
B		Oldtown				Taunton		
C	Hutton			Bourneville		Peaceton		Exmere
D			Johnton			Marsden	Sawbridge	
E		Tonbridge		Carville				Newtown
F			Littleworth		Baxton			
		Helsinki			Barton	Persing		
G		Jamestown		Richville				
			Reddinton		Aston			
H	Onnington							

CODE 5.7

For each of the following sets of place-names, use a pencil to join the place-names in the order given, using the map above. What letter is revealed for each set of places, and what word is spelled out? After revealing each letter, erase your lines so that you can decode the following letters.

- Tonbridge Reddinton Aston Peaceton Taunton (marked on the map as an example)
- Bourneville Peaceton Sawbridge Persing Aston Reddinton Helsinki Johnton Bourneville
- Mersey Littleworth
- Reddinton Bourneville Aston Peaceton
- Peaceton Bourneville Littleworth Baxton Littleworth Reddinton Aston
- Hutton Johnton Jamestown Onnington Hutton

< / WRITE THE MESSAGE HERE / >

J _____   _____   _____   _____   _____   _____

ANOTHER WAY TO MAKE A MESSAGE HARDER TO CRACK—instead of combining both a code and a picture, such as a map—is to combine two different visual codes. Not many people can read both pigpen and Cruz's mom's spiral code, for example.

CODE 5.8

Decode the following phrase that uses two of the visual codes you learned earlier in this chapter:

< / WRITE YOUR PHRASE HERE / >

{ HUBBARD'S HINT } SOME OF THE SYMBOLS HAVE BEEN MOVED CLOSER TOGETHER SO THAT THEY NEARLY OVERLAP, BUT THIS DOESN'T CHANGE HOW YOU READ THEM. SOME ARE IN PIGPEN, AND SOME ARE IN CRUZ'S MOM'S SPIRAL CODE.

AS YOU EXIT THE MAP ROOM, YOU NOTICE A PILE OF COINS ON THE FLOOR. WHAT COULD IT MEAN? Instead of drawing the symbols that make up visual codes, you could hide them in pictures—or represent the symbols in some other way. For example, you could arrange coins to hide a pigpen message by using them to represent the pigpen grids (as shown on page 82) instead.

For the A-to-I grid, start with a 3 x 3 arrangement of coins, all heads up. Then flip one to tails to indicate a letter in a particular position. To represent the J-to-R grid, start with all tails up and then just flip one to heads. So the letter F would look like this (below, left), and the letter P like this (below, right)—notice how the heads and tails are reversed between the two pictures.

LETTER F

A	B	C
D	E	F
G	H	I

LETTER P

J	K	L
M	N	O
P	Q	R

The last two grids, for S to V and for W to Z, work in a similar way except that the coins are placed in a diamond formation. For the S-to-V grid, start with all coins heads up, and for W to Z start with them all tails up—then flip the coin in the position of the letter you want. For example, the letter S looks like this (below, left), and the letter Z like this (below, right):

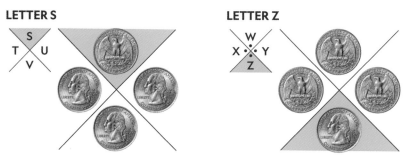

LETTER S

LETTER Z

CODE 5.9

Using the pigpen coin code, decode the following message in the coins you found. Each line is a different word.

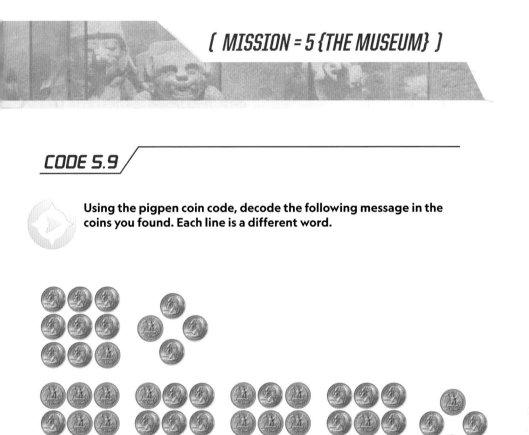

< / WRITE THE MESSAGE HERE / >

YOU'RE ALMOST DONE, but you notice some odd words on a bulletin board near the exit. Could these be the final codes? A completely different way to write a secret message is to use normal English letters but to write them in a way that makes them hard to read. Try the messages here and see how you do!

CODE 5.10

Can you decode the following message, in which each letter has been changed in the same way?

P!SⱵ!6∩⅃ED

< / WRITE THE MESSAGE HERE / >

 { HUBBARD'S HINT } TRY ROTATING EACH LETTER BY THE SAME AMOUNT. THERE IS ALSO A MIX OF UPPERCASE AND LOWERCASE LETTERS, TO MAKE IT TRICKIER.

CODE 5.11

Can you decode the following message, in which each letter has been changed in the same way?

< / WRITE THE MESSAGE HERE / >

ANOTHER WAY TO CONCEAL LETTERS is to write them on top of one another.

CODE 5.12

In this picture, the letters of a word have been written so that they overlap with the next letter in the word. Overlapped areas are black. Can you read the original word?

< / WRITE THE WORD HERE / >

You can also overlap pieces of text completely. This works best with colored letters, since with a bit of practice you can make your eyes pay attention only to one color of word at a time.

CODE 5.13

Two words have been written on top of each other in this picture. Can you figure out what each word is?

< / WRITE THE WORDS HERE / >

{ HUBBARD'S HINT } ONE WORD STARTS WITH H, AND THE OTHER STARTS WITH P.

WELL DONE, EXPLORER–

YOU'VE COMPLETED ALL OF THE VISUAL CODE TESTS YOU ENCOUNTERED IN THE MUSEUM.

Now it's time to find out your next—and final—destination along this codebreaking scavenger hunt. To do this, you'll have shade in some of the regions in the boxes below. Once you're done, they'll spell out the name of your next location. Remember that even master codebreakers can't crack every code! If you don't have all the answers you need, you can always check the solutions at the back of the book.

CODE 5.14

Notice how each of the boxes has some grid lines on it? These grid lines are the same lines that were used to define the pigpen cipher back on page 82. In this puzzle, you'll shade in the boxes that correspond to the location of certain letters. Sounds complex? It isn't! For example, if you wanted to shade in the D area and then shade in the Y area, you would shade like this:

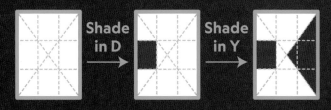

Shade in D

Shade in Y

{ HUBBARD'S HINT } CHECK BACK TO PAGE 82 TO SEE WHY THESE ARE THE D AND Y AREAS, IF YOU NEED TO!

 Shade in boxes based on the following letters. Some boxes won't require any shading.

Boxes 1 and 6: From code 5.2, shade the middle letter of the second word of the answer.

Box 2: From code 5.9, shade the third and fourth letters of the second word of the answer.

Box 4: From code 5.1, shade the first letter of the second word, the first two letters of the fourth word, and the middle letter of the last word of the answer.

Box 5: From code 5.5, shade the first letter of the answer.

Box 7: From code 5.11, shade the middle two letters of the first word and the middle two letters of the second word.

Boxes 8 and 16: From code 5.10, shade the first and fourth letters.

Boxes 10 and 13: From code 5.7, shade the fifth letter of the answer.

Box 11: From code 5.3, shade the first, third, fourth, and fifth letters of the final word of the answer.

Boxes 14 and 15: From code 5.8, shade the third letter of the first word of the answer.

Box 17: From code 5.6, shade the middle letter of the first word of the answer.

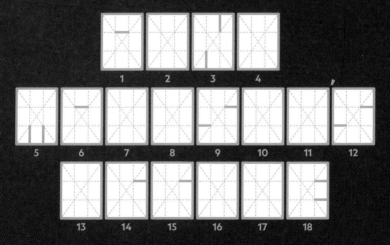

Now look at the resulting shaded boxes. Can you read your next destination?

<AUNT MARISOL'S OFFICE>

Welcome to the last mission of the scavenger hunt.

Dr. Marisol Coronado (also known as Cruz's aunt Marisol) is away from her desk, but she's left a stack of papers for you. This professor of anthropology and paleontology at the Academy is also a cryptology expert, so you know you're going to need to be on your game. On top is a sticky note with a message:

You take a look at the papers. Each one is a challenge using a different code—or codes—that you've encountered earlier in the hunt.

Congratulations, explorer! Think you can remember how to crack the codes and solve the puzzles you tackled along the way? It's time to find out!

MISSION=6

Aunt Marisol's office

/ CODE 6.1 /

THE FIRST PAGE IN THE STACK is a letter from Aunt Marisol:

There must be a hidden message in this letter! What is it?

Dear Explorer,

I am so proud to hear that you have been able to <u>check</u> off all of the puzzles so far! As I look <u>back</u> over them, I am impressed <u>to</u> learn that you have solved all of the <u>earlier</u> tests. These last <u>pages</u> will test what you have learned. So <u>if</u> you are ready to continue, let's start!

Oh—and if <u>you</u> do <u>need</u> a clue at any point, read the sticky notes I have left on each page. These will <u>help</u> you solve each puzzle.

Good luck!

Dr. Marisol Coronado

Let me <u>underline</u> my message— these sticky notes provide clues!

< / WRITE THE HIDDEN MESSAGE HERE / >

> **AHA, THE SECRET WAS TO READ THE UNDERLINED WORDS**—just like the very first message that started your scavenger hunt! The next page in Aunt Marisol's pile contains a letter from three of Cruz's closest friends:

Dear Dr. Coronado,

You won't believe what we found! We can't write down the details, but we think it will help Cruz on his mission. Let's meet in person. Does our suggested appointment time work for you?

Sincerely,

EMMETT   Bryndis

Sailor

Interesting decorations on this letter—PP?

{ HUBBARD'S HINT } STUCK? SEE PAGE 83 FOR HELP.

The letter refers to meeting at a "suggested appointment time," but there's no appointment time given in the text of the letter.

You realize ... the letter must contain another hidden code! But where? You look at Aunt Marisol's sticky note, which mentions the decorative borders. Hmmm. Are there changes in the border pattern that remind you of something you've seen before? And could "PP" be shorthand for the name of a code?

CODE 6.2

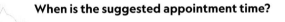

When is the suggested appointment time?

< / WRITE THE TIME HERE / >

SNEAKY! THE CODE WAS HIDDEN IN THE DESIGN at the top and bottom of the page. You'd better keep your eyes peeled for more hidden codes, explorer.

The next page in the stack contains some math calculations:

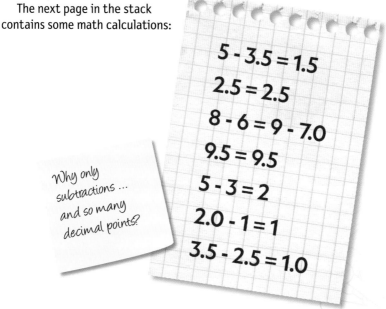

$$5 - 3.5 = 1.5$$
$$2.5 = 2.5$$
$$8 - 6 = 9 - 7.0$$
$$9.5 = 9.5$$
$$5 - 3 = 2$$
$$2.0 - 1 = 1$$
$$3.5 - 2.5 = 1.0$$

Why only subtractions ... and so many decimal points?

CODE 6.3

There's no text—just the calculations. What could this mean? Perhaps, like on the previous page, some of the content is a distraction and only certain parts of it contain the actual code?

< / WRITE THE HIDDEN WORD HERE / >

{ HUBBARD'S HINT } STUCK? SEE IF THE CODE ON PAGE 46 CAN HELP.

▷ **YOU FLIP TO THE NEXT PAGE** and see that it contains a short passage:

> As you solve these
> codes, make sure you
> remember to use all
> of the skills you have
> newly learned as
> you worked through
> my previous codes!

Those lines are so short—is this some kind of poem?

CODE 6.4

Could there be a hidden message here? ... Or a hidden word?

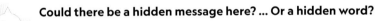

< / WRITE THE HIDDEN WORD HERE / >

🐾 { HUBBARD'S HINT } STUCK? PAGE 16 SHOULD BE ABLE TO HELP YOU OUT.

MOVING ON TO THE NEXT PAGE IN THE STACK, you see illustrations of colorful flags. Below them is a simple question. Can you answer it?

W 🇮🇳 🇩🇰 ⚑ ⚑ N 🇪🇸 🇳🇴 🇳🇴

⚑ O ⚑ ⚑ ⚑

⚑ ⚑ 🇰🇪 ⚑ 🇹🇹 🇦🇷

What do flags need?

Countries ...
then states?

CODE 6.5

You've seen country flags used for a message before—but why does the sticky note refer to states, too? Once you decode the flags, is there another step you should take? (Don't forget that states have abbreviations!)

< / WRITE THE HIDDEN WORD HERE / >

ONE OF THE FLAGS ON THE LEFT BELONGS TO BRYNDIS'S HOME COUNTRY, ICELAND. THE RED IS SAID TO SYMBOLIZE ACTIVE VOLCANOES; THE WHITE, ICE AND SNOW; AND THE BLUE, THE OCEAN.

{ HUBBARD'S HINT } STUCK? YOU'LL NEED TO CHECK OUT PAGES 54 AND 56—THERE ARE TWO STEPS TO SOLVING THIS CODE!

▶ **ON THE NEXT PAGE, YOU FIND AN IMAGE OF A COMPASS** accompanied by directions. Where do the directions lead? There's not much space in the office to actually move around ... could it be another code?

Each pair of compass directions decodes to one letter.

1. W and SE
2. NE and S
3. SW and E
4. SW and S
5. W and N

6. W and SW
7. W and NW
8. W and E
9. S and NE

IN VERY EARLY COMPASSES, A MAGNETIZED NEEDLE WAS ATTACHED TO A PIECE OF WOOD OR CORK FLOATING IN A DISH OF WATER.

CODE 6.6

You realize that this list of compass directions must be concealing a nine-letter word!

< / WRITE THE HIDDEN WORD HERE / >

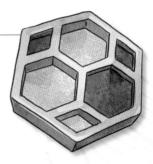

 { HUBBARD'S HINT } STUCK? THE CODE ON PAGE 50 WILL SHOW YOU THE WAY!

NICE WORK, EXPLORER—YOU'RE ON A ROLL! Turning to the next page, you see a screen capture of a text exchange. It looks as if someone was having a conversation with Dr. Kira Benedict, professor of art and journalism at the Academy:

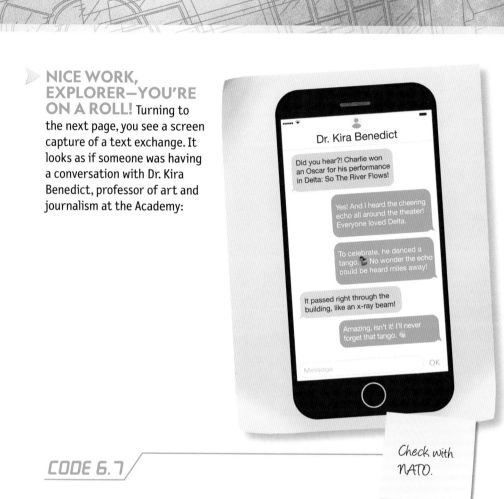

Dr. Kira Benedict

Did you hear?! Charlie won an Oscar for his performance in Delta: So The River Flows!

Yes! And I heard the cheering echo all around the theater! Everyone loved Delta.

To celebrate, he danced a tango. No wonder the echo could be heard miles away!

It passed right through the building, like an x-ray beam!

Amazing, isn't it! I'll never forget that tango.

Message   OK

CODE 6.7

Check with NATO.

You know by now that this isn't just a conversation—it's a code! Time to get cracking.

< /WRITE THE HIDDEN TWO-WORD PHRASE HERE / >

{ HUBBARD'S HINT } STUCK? PAGE 60 WILL REVEAL WHAT TO LOOK FOR.

THE STACK OF PAPER IS STARTING TO FEEL MUCH SMALLER—it looks like you're nearly finished, explorer! There are just two more pages after this one:

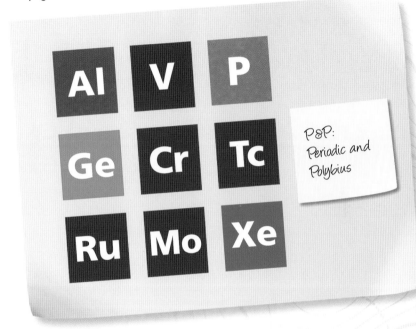

P&P:
Periodic and
Polybius

CODE 6.8

You've seen boxed letters like these before! But where? Aunt Marisol's note referring to P&P has to be a clue. Of course! She must know about your detour into the Synthesis! Since there are two P's, could there also be two stages to decoding this message?

< / WRITE THE HIDDEN WORD HERE / >

{ HUBBARD'S HINT } STUCK? START WITH PAGES 68 AND 69, THEN TURN TO PAGE 38.

THE NEXT-TO-LAST PAGE ISN'T ON A PIECE OF PAPER, but a very thin slab of wood, almost like an ancient artifact! Carved into it are various curved shapes:

Spirals ... and an A-to-Z reversal?

CODE 6.9

These spirals look very familiar. Hmm ... this should be easy, right? Knowing Aunt Marisol—probably not! It looks like decoding this one will require two steps, as well.

< / WRITE THE HIDDEN TWO-WORD PHRASE HERE / >

{ HUBBARD'S HINT } START WITH THE CODE ON PAGE 86, THEN APPLY THE CODE FROM PAGE 34.

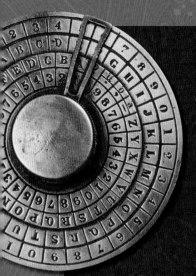

THIS IS IT,
EXPLORER–

YOU'RE AT THE END OF THE SCAVENGER HUNT! You have made your way around the Academy, cracking codes and solving puzzles.

CODE 6.10

 Beneath the wooden board is a small scroll. You unroll it to find just one last message to reveal, using the answers you've uncovered to the puzzles in Aunt Marisol's office:

WORD 1

☐ = sixth letter of the hidden word in code 6.4

☐ = seventh letter of the hidden word in code 6.6

☐ = second letter of the first word of the hidden message in code 6.2

WORD 2

☐ = **third letter of the first word of the hidden phrase in code 6.7**

☐ = **third letter of the first word of the hidden phrase in code 6.9**

☐ = **first letter of the hidden word in code 6.3**

WORD 3

☐ = **second letter of the hidden word in code 6.5**

☐ = **seventh letter of the hidden word in code 6.8**

Copy WORDS 1, 2, and 3 into the spaces below, to reveal the final message:

WORD 1   WORD 2   WORD 3

Once you've decoded the message, turn the page to claim your prize.

< / WRITE THE THREE-WORD MESSAGE HERE / >

**EXPLORER
ACADEMY**

Well done, recruit!

You have successfully completed all missions of the annual explorer scavenger hunt (including one diversion *underground* you cleverly worked your way out of).

You put your skills to the test and *found* the solutions to some very tricky codes that, in *truth,* could have confounded even the most confident cryptographer. Let this *be* a lesson: As Nellie Bly believed, "Energy rightly applied and directed will accomplish anything."

Please accept *the* certificate of successful completion on the opposite page as your first official document as a full-fledged student at Explorer Academy.

I look forward to our future adventures together. Now that you've proven yourself, we know we can entrust you with the most confidential information. And for recruits seeking further clues about Cruz's momentous mission, remember: Codes revealing secret messages *can* be found anywhere—even here. Onward!

Cordially,

Regina M. Hightower, Ph.D.

Explorer Academy President

CERTIFICATE OF ACHIEVEMENT

stating that

_____

(your name here)

has successfully navigated the
ANNUAL EXPLORER SCAVENGER HUNT,
a unique challenge of complex codes
and elaborate puzzles,

and that from

_____

(today's date)

forward promises to uphold the highest
standards of integrity, honesty, and compassion,
as well as the cornerstone ideals on
which the Academy was founded:

***WITH ALL, COOPERATION. FOR ALL,
RESPECT. ABOVE ALL, HONOR.***

Regina M. Hightower, Ph.D.
Explorer Academy President

INTRODUCTION

CODE 1.1 / PG. 8
Read just the underlined words to reveal the hidden message: "Your journey will start in the library."

MISSION ONE

CODE 1.2 / PG. 11
The italicized words reveal "Congratulations on cracking your first code. Now read the next page."

CODE 1.3 / PG. 12
The last words of each sentence together spell "final letter in alphabet."

CODE 1.4 / PG. 13
The first words spell out "What is the fifth vowel?"

CODE 1.5 / PG. 14
The words spell out "Which letter sounds most like see?"

CODE 1.6 / PG. 15
The highlighted words spell "reverse the letters of the word."

CODE 1.7 / PG. 16
Read together, in order, the first letters of each line spell out "What is the thirteenth letter?"

CODE 1.8 / PG. 17
The message reads "Secret codes have often been used to send important messages during times of war."

CODE 1.9 / PG. 18
The message reads "Can you tell me what the middle letter of the word 'art' is?"

CODE 1.10 / PG. 19
The message reads, "You are becoming a master codebreaker! An expert on codes is called a cryptographer."

CODE 1.11 / PG. 20
The message reads "Which letter of the alphabet looks most like a perfect circle?"

CODE 1.12 / PG. 21
The hidden phrase is "What is the nineteenth letter of the alphabet?"

CODE 1.13 / PG. 22
1. Antelope, 2. Parrot, 3. Ostrich, 4. Sheep, 5. Tiger, 6. Reindeer, 7. Octopus, 8. Penguin, 9. Horse, 10. Elephant

The 10-letter word that can be read down the initial letters is APOSTROPHE.

CODE 1.14 / PG. 23
Swap the first and last letter of each word, to reveal "It was the codebreaking skills of top cryptographers that helped the Allies to win the Second World War."

SOLUTIONS

CODE 1.15 / PG. 24

Reverse the order of all except the first and last letters of each word to reveal "What is the third consonant in the English alphabet?"

CODE 1.16 / PG. 25

The message reads, "What letter appears third most frequently in this phrase?"

CODE 1.17 / PG. 27

The first word is CRUZ'S, the second word is DORM, and the third word is MOOR. Once you reverse the letters of the third word as per the instruction on page 15, you end up with CRUZ'S DORM ROOM.

MISSION TWO

CODE 2.1 / PG. 29

The text reads, "It can take two months to climb Mount Everest!"

CODE 2.2 / PG. 30

The messages reads, "The youngest person to climb Mount Everest was thirteen-year-old Jordan Romero."

CODE 2.3 / PG. 31

The message has a forward shift of five, and reads, "The oldest person to climb Mount Everest was eighty-year-old Yuichiro Miura."

CODE 2.4 / PG. 33

The decoded message reads, "Mice rule the world."

CODE 2.5 / PG. 33

The decoded message reads, "Mount Everest crosses the border between China and Nepal."

CODE 2.6 / PG. 34

The decoded message reads, "Mount Everest is known as Sagarmatha in the Nepali language."

CODE 2.7 / PG. 35

The decoded message reads, "Mount Everest is called Chomolungma in the Tibetan language." *Chomolungma* means "Goddess Mother of the World."

CODE 2.8 / PG. 37

The encoded message is BRSSEAEFPEWOI, which you can extract from the completed table:

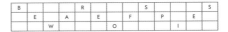

B			R			S			S
	E	A		E	F	P		E	
		W			O			I	

The decoded message reads, "Everest is about 29,000 feet high," which you can extract from the completed table:

CODE 2.9 / PG. 39

"Danger is all around" is encoded as
14 11 33 22 15 42 24 43 11 31 31
11 42 34 45 33 14.

CODE 2.10 / PG. 39

The secret answer is "Tenzing Norgay and Edmund Hillary."

CODE 2.11 / PG. 41

The message reads, "The first ascent of Everest was in 1953."

CODE 2.12 / PG. 42

"What do Mount Everest and a jumbo jet have in common?"

CODE 2.13 / PG. 43

The decoded message reads, "Their wind speed and take-off speed are sometimes the same!"

CODE 2.14 / PG. 45

WORD ONE: The first word decodes from 22 43 51 to GSV, and that then decodes to THE. **WORD TWO:** The second word is CAVE. So the destination is THE CAVE.

MISSION THREE

CODE 3.1 / PG. 47
EXPLORE

CODE 3.2 / PG. 48
A TELEGRAPH MESSAGE

CODE 3.3 / PG. 49

CRUZ. In Morse code, this is "dash dot dash dot," "dot dash dot," "dot dot dash," "dash dash dot dot." Here's how it looks in the main paragraph of the message, with dashes and dots in bold highlighter:

Don't tell me; you're sitting under the veran**da sh**ade, counting the **dot**s on the cloth and waiting to **dash** off to Orlan**do t**his weekend. I know you're sick of having to cook and clean and **do t**he laundry, and a trip to Flori**da sh**ould be a good anti**dot**e to your boredom. If you haven't gone shopping yet, I think you should ditch those boring old avoca**do t**ops you always wear for a pair of funky, polka-**dot** pan**da sh**irts. You would look more **dash**ing, beyond **a sh**adow of a doubt, and **ot**her people would have to **do t**heir best not to stare—which is always amusing!

CODE 3.4 / PG. 51
FLY THE FLAG

CODE 3.5 / PG. 52
TIME TO LEARN SEMAPHORE

CODE 3.6 / PG. 53
DOUBLE STRENGTH

CODE 3.7 / PG. 55

The flags spell out "DENMARK HAS THE OLDEST FLAG"—which it does! It dates back to 1625.

CODE 3.8 / PG. 57
IN CODE LAND

CODE 3.9 / PG. 59
THE SPY IS NEAR

CODE 3.10 / PG. 61
NICE JOB. In the NATO phonetic alphabet, this is NOVEMBER, INDIA, CHARLIE, ECHO, JULIET, OSCAR, and BRAVO, which is obtained from:

November 2017

*A Passage to **India**,* adapted for the stage by director/playwright **Charlie** Lopez, is a visually stunning, emotionally charged theatrical hit. Lopez's script, although it contains a strong **echo** of Forster's original prose, gives the dialogue a modern twist, and is in equal parts humorous and heart-wrenching. In terms of the cast, lead actress **Juliet** Tarskaya is a standout as Mrs. Moore. Many have doubted whether Tarskaya would be able to translate her on-screen presence to the stage, but the **Oscar** nominee gives everything to this role, and is sure to silence the critics. **Bravo**!

CODE 3.11 / PG. 63
WORD ONE: The secret message in code 3.4 is FLY THE FLAG, so THE is the second word.
WORD TWO:
- The oldest flag is that of DENMARK, so the middle letter is M.
- ..- decodes via Morse code to U.
- Code 3.6 decoded to DOUBLE STRENGTH, so the thing that was "double" is STRENGTH, making this answer S.
- The decoded message in 3.1 is EXPLORE, which starts and ends with the letter E.
- 10:10 can be read, in semaphore, as two flags held up at opposite diagonals, making the letter U.
- Three taps of your finger, in the code given on pages 58 and 59, makes M.
So the location is THE MUSEUM.

CODE 4.1 / PG. 65
The red (top) button opens the door.

CODE 4.2 / PG. 66

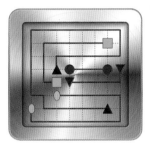

CODE 4.3 / PG. 67

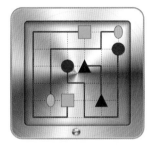

CODE 4.4 / PG. 69
The numbers are atomic numbers of elements. The abbreviations for those elements are 89=Ac, 22=Ti, 23=V, 85=At, 53=I, 8=O, and 7=N. Taken together, these spell ACTIVATION, the required password.

CODE 4.5 / PG. 70
ATTENTION must be split into the elements At, Te, N, Ti, O, and N. Their atomic numbers are 85, 52, 7, 22, 8, and 7, making the access code 855272287.

CODE 4.6 / PG. 71

Each set of numbers traces out a path along the periodic table, making the shape of a number. The first number is 5 and the second number is 9, making the access code 59.

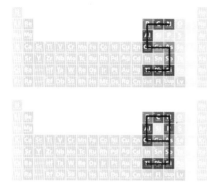

CODE 4.7 / PG. 73

The most direct way to do it:

- Pour C into A, to give 3-0-7 (in A-B-C)
- Pour A into B, to give 0-3-7
- Pour C into A, to give 3-3-4
- Pour A into B, to give 0-6-4
- Pour C into A, to give 3-6-1
- Pour A into B, to give 2-7-1
- Pour B into C, to give 2-0-8—and you are done, since C now contains 8 liters

CODE 4.8 / PG. 74

24 oz = 3 oz + 10 oz + 11 oz

CODE 4.9 / PG. 75

27 oz = 7 oz + 8 oz + 12 oz
34 oz = 3 oz + 8 oz + 11 oz + 12 oz
39 oz = 3 oz + 7 oz + 8 oz + 10 oz + 11 oz

CODE 4.10 / PG. 76

LEAVE IN EXACTLY NINE MINUTES

CODE 4.11 / PG. 77

START is 19-20-1-18-20.

CODE 4.12 / PG. 79

- Start both timers at once.
- Then, once the 5-minute timer has finished, turn it back over immediately.
- Next, once the 7-minute timer has finished, turn the 5-minute timer back over even though it hasn't yet finished. Two minutes will have passed since you started it, so it will take two more minutes to reverse this process. This will allow you to time 2 more minutes after the 7-minute timer ends, for a total of 9 minutes.
- Once the 5-minute timer finishes its 2 minutes of sand, exactly 9 minutes of time will have passed. Success!

CODE 4.13 / PG. 81

Tracing out the numbered elements on the periodic table reveals the letters F and E. If you read them together, you have FE.

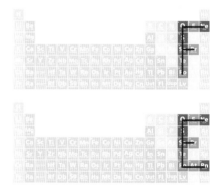

Looking in the periodic table you find the entry Fe, whose atomic number is 26. So 26 is the code you need for the door. (Although F is an element, there is no element represented by E, but good work if you tried to use F=9 as the first of the two digits!)

SOLUTIONS

MISSION FIVE

CODE 5.1 / PG. 83
THE PEN IS MIGHTIER THAN THE SWORD

CODE 5.2 / PG. 84
PRESS THE SPACE BAR

CODE 5.3 / PG. 85
The pigpen translates to UORK GSV YZXLM. When an Atbash cipher is applied, it becomes FLIP THE BACON.

CODE 5.4 / PG. 87
FOLLOWING YOU AROUND

CODE 5.5 / PG. 89
From left-to-right, the hieroglyphic values are O=1,010,101; E=32,000; D=40; L=300,021; S=2,000,000; V=122,200. When sorted into decreasing order, this spells out SOLVED.

CODE 5.6 / PG. 91
Take the first letter of the town in each grid square. The exact position of each town is identified by the blue dots. The solution reads NOT TO SCALE.

CODE 5.7 / PG. 92
JOINED

CODE 5.8 / PG. 93
CURLY TAILS

CODE 5.9 / PG. 95
IT MAKES CENTS

CODE 5.10 / PG. 96
Rotate each letter by 180 degrees to reveal DISFIGURED.

CODE 5.11 / PG. 96
LEFT BEHIND

CODE 5.12 / PG. 97
READABLE

CODE 5.13 / PG. 97
HIDDEN PHRASE

CODE 5.14 / PG. 99
When shaded as described, the boxes will look like this:

They spell out "Aunt Marisol's office" ... your next location!"

MISSION SIX

CODE 6.1 / PG. 101

As the sticky note hints, the underlined words are important. If you read them, you reveal a hidden message: "Check back to earlier pages if you need help."

CODE 6.2 / PG. 103

PP = pigpen! Pigpen code is hidden in the decorative border, in each of the square boxes. There is one word across the top, and three words at the bottom—two spiral patterns without a square box between them represent a space. The message therefore reads:

CODE 6.3 / PG. 104

-..	D
..	I
--.	G
..	I
-	T
.-	A
.-..	L

So the hidden word is DIGITAL.

CODE 6.4 / PG. 105

The first letters of each line form an acronym, spelling out the answer: ACRONYM.

CODE 6.5 / PG. 107

Keep the given letters and replace each flag with the initial letter of the country it represents. This then spells:
- WISCONSIN
- NORTH DAKOTA

Replace each of these with its state abbreviation, to make:
- WI
- ND

Together these form a single word, which is what flags need: WIND.

CODE 6.6 / PG. 109

This code works just like the clock face code (code 3.5 on page 52), but with compass points instead of a clock face. Every combination of directions represents a semaphore flag in which each arm is pointing to one of the two directions, so every pair of directions can be read as a semaphore letter. The first one, pointing W and SE, represents the letter S. Decoding the rest reveals the answer: SEMAPHORE.

CODE 6.7 / PG. 110

As the sticky note suggests, it is the NATO alphabet. In among the other words are the following: Charlie Oscar Delta echo Delta tango echo x-ray tango. These spell out CODED TEXT, the answer.

CODE 6.8 / PG. 111

The boxes represent elements in the periodic table. Start by converting each element to its atomic number: Al = 13; V = 23; P = 15; Ge = 32; Cr = 24; Tc = 43; Ru = 44; Mo = 42; Xe = 54.
Now use the Polybius square to convert each number to a letter. This will reveal the answer: CHEMISTRY.

CODE 6.9 / PG. 113

The shapes around the outside of the board represent the spiral code and look like this:

The spiral code reads HKRIZORMT ZILFMW. The tip refers to the Atbash cipher on page 34. Applying the Atbash cipher to these letters reveals the solution: SPIRALING AROUND.

CODE 6.10 / PG. 115

The three words are: YOU DID IT. And indeed you did. Congratulations, explorer! You truly are a master codebreaker.

PHOTO CREDITS

For more information, visit nationalgeographic.com, call 1-877-873-6846, or write to the following address:

National Geographic Partners
1145 17th Street N.W.
Washington, D.C. 20036-4688 U.S.A.

Visit us online at nationalgeographic.com/books

For librarians and teachers:
nationalgeographic.com/books/librarians-and-educators

More for kids from National Geographic:
natgeokids.com

National Geographic Kids magazine inspires children to explore their world with fun yet educational articles on animals, science, nature, and more. Using fresh storytelling and amazing photography, *Nat Geo Kids* shows kids ages 6 to 14 the fascinating truth about the world—and why they should care. **kids.nationalgeographic.com/subscribe**

Since 1888, the National Geographic Society has funded more than 12,000 research, exploration, and preservation projects around the world. The Society receives funds from National Geographic Partners, LLC, funded in part by your purchase. A portion of the proceeds from this book supports this vital work. To learn more, visit natgeo.com/info.

For rights or permissions inquiries, please contact National Geographic Books Subsidiary Rights: bookrights@natgeo.com

Designed by Rachael Hamm Plett, Moduza Design

ISBN: 978-1-4263-3307-1

The publisher would like to thank Becky Baines, editorial director; Paige Towler, associate editor; Jen Agresta, project editor; Eva Absher, art director; Lori Epstein, photo editor; Alix Inchausti, production editor; and Anne LeongSon and Gus Tello, design production assistants.

Printed in the United States of America
20/VP/2

EXPL⬥RER ACADEMY

GET IN ON THE ADVENTURE!

Were you there for Cruz's first day at Explorer Academy? Start at the beginning. Meet Cruz, Lani, Emmett, and Sailor, and discover why Explorer Academy is the coolest school on the planet in *The Nebula Secret* and *The Falcon's Feather* ... and beyond! Get the story behind Cruz's mysterious mission, practice your new codebreaking skills, and explore the world!

"A fun, exciting, and action-packed ride that kids will love." —J.J. ABRAMS

"Inspires the next generation of curious kids to go out into our world and discover something unexpected." —JAMES CAMERON

EXPL⬥RER ACADEMY
THE NEBULA SECRET
A NOVEL

TRUDI TRUEIT

"I promise: Once you enter Explorer Academy, you'll never want to leave." —Valerie Tripp, co-creator and author of the American Girl series

EXPL⬥RER ACADEMY
THE FALCON'S FEATHER
A NOVEL

TRUDI TRUEIT

UNDER THE *Stars*

NATIONAL GEOGRAPHIC

AVAILABLE WHEREVER BOOKS ARE SOLD
View the video and discover more at ExplorerAcademy.com